 Robin Lee Hatcher and available from
Point Large Print:

trayal
Promise Kept

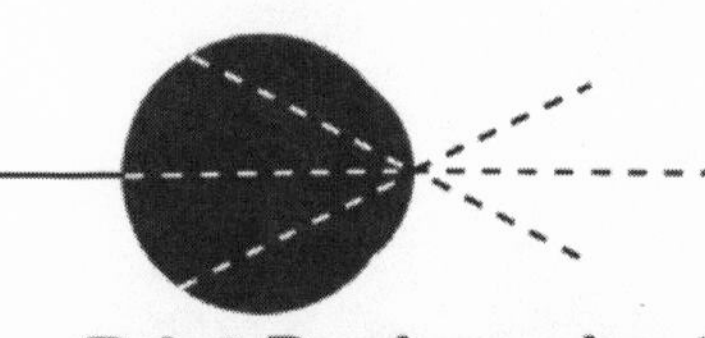

This Large Print Book carries the Seal of Approval of N.A.V.H.

The

Hear
Purs

Also b
Cente

The Heart's Pursuit

Robin Lee Hatcher

Center Point Large Print
Thorndike, Maine

This Center Point Large Print edition is published in the year 2014 by arrangement with Zondervan.

The text of this Large Print edition is unabridged.
In other aspects, this book may vary from the original edition.
Printed in the United States of America on permanent paper.
Set in 16-point Times New Roman type.

ISBN: 978-1-62899-175-8

Library of Congress Cataloging-in-Publication Data

Hatcher, Robin Lee.
The Heart's pursuit / Robin Lee Hatcher. —
Center Point Large Print edition.
pages ; cm
Summary: "Two wounded hearts—a beauty abandoned at the altar and a rugged bounty hunter—join forces in a pursuit across the Old West"—Provided by publisher.
ISBN 978-1-62899-175-8 (library binding : alk. paper)
1. Bounty hunters—Fiction. 2. Fugitives from justice—Fiction.
3. Large type books. I. Title.
PS3558.A73574H44 2014b
813′.54—dc23

2014015769

Never take your own revenge, beloved, but leave room for the wrath of God, for it is written, "VENGEANCE IS MINE, I WILL REPAY," says the Lord.

—ROMANS 12:19

Chapter 1

May 1873

Bright sunlight glared down on the small town of Twin Springs, Colorado, as Jared Newman stopped his pinto gelding in front of the saloon. Silence reigned along the main street. If he hadn't ridden through here three days earlier, he would have thought the town abandoned. Not a soul in sight.

He removed his battered Stetson and raked his fingers through his hair, then stepped down from the saddle. He knocked the hat against his pant leg a few times, shaking loose the trail dust. He was bone weary, and his temper had seen better days. The latter was due to the unseasonable heat. The former was due to the man who rode with him.

"Get down, Peterson. We could both use something to drink."

His prisoner obeyed, sliding to the ground, his wrists cuffed in front of him.

With a jingle of spurs, Jared ushered Lute Peterson through the swinging doors of the Mountain Rose Saloon. The narrow room was dimly lit and musty smelling. Two men, a circle of smoke lingering above their heads, glanced up from their game of cards. A blonde in a dress that might have been the height of fashion a decade or two earlier lounged against the bar.

Behind her, the bartender swirled a white cloth along the bar's hardwood surface. He grinned at the new customers, but his expression changed fast enough when he noticed the cuffs on Peterson's wrists. His gaze shifted to Jared. "What'll it be?"

"Sarsaparilla. Two." He tossed some coins onto the bar.

Peterson cast a look of disbelief in Jared's direction. "*Sarsaparilla?* How about a whiskey?"

Jared ignored him.

The woman sidled closer. "Haven't seen you in here before. Where you headed? Or are you new to town?"

He glanced at her. A generous dusting of powder and rouge had been applied to her angular face. Like her dress, she might have been attractive at one time, but life had left its mark around her eyes and in the cynical corners of her painted mouth.

When he didn't answer, she smirked. "Cat got your tongue?"

He would prefer to ignore her question the way he had Peterson's request for hard liquor, but he had a feeling she wouldn't leave him alone until he answered. "I'm taking my prisoner to Denver."

The bartender set the two glasses on the bar. Jared grabbed one and brought it to his lips, draining the drink in one long gulp.

"You a lawman?" the woman asked.

"Of a sort." He tossed another coin onto the bar. "I'll have another one."

"You look tired, mister. You should stay in town for the night." She leaned closer, smiling an invitation.

Jared caught a whiff of her cheap cologne and grimaced. "Sorry. We're in a hurry."

"I ain't in no hurry." Peterson grinned as if he were a friend instead of a common thief headed for jail. "I'd stay with the lady if she wants company."

With a shake of his head, Jared addressed the bartender again. "Where is everyone? The town looks deserted."

"Big wedding over at the church." The man poured Jared another sarsaparilla. "Our fair town's leading family's got a daughter getting hitched. Just about everybody's there."

"But none of you went." Jared tossed back this drink the same way he had the first.

The blonde at his elbow laughed. "Do we look like the type to get invited to a church weddin'?" She snorted.

Jared shrugged, then looked toward Peterson. "Let's go."

"Why don't we spend the night here, like the

lady asked?" He grabbed his glass and downed the drink. "Ain't you tired?"

Jared took hold of Peterson's left arm and steered him out of the saloon. "Mount up. We've got a lot of ground to cover before dark."

Too bad Twin Springs didn't have a sheriff—something he'd learned when he passed through the town the last time. It would suit Jared just fine not to have to ride into Denver to collect his reward. He'd like to be done with Peterson.

As they stepped toward the horses, Jared's hand still gripping Peterson's arm, he glanced in the opposite direction—and stopped dead in his tracks. A young woman raced toward him, a vision in white satin and pearls, her long lace train dragging on the dusty planks of the boardwalk. As he watched, she jerked the filmy veil from her head and sent her ebony hair cascading down her back, then tossed the headdress into the street.

Undoubtedly the daughter of the aforementioned leading family of Twin Springs. But a happy bride she was not. What had caused her to flee the church? A case of cold feet, perhaps. If so, they must be frigid indeed. Despite himself, an amused grin crept into the corners of his mouth.

At that moment, the fleeing bride seemed to become aware of the two men standing in the street beside their horses. She came to a stop on the boardwalk, and her eyes lifted to meet Jared's. Silver-gray in a pretty face, they were awash with tears and filled with pain. His amusement vanished.

"We going or not, bounty?" Peterson demanded.

The woman's eyes widened a fraction before she continued past them in a flash of white, disappearing moments later around the next corner.

Jared was sorry she'd seen his grin. He regretted finding levity in her apparent sorrow—whatever the cause of it. "We're going." He gave Peterson a little push toward his mount.

The sooner they made Denver, the happier Jared would be.

Chapter 2

Silver Matlock sat on the edge of the settee, staring at the carpet, her hands balled into tight fists in her lap. Tension gripped the small parlor, as it had gripped the house ever since her disastrous would-be wedding six days earlier.

"Are you telling me we could lose the store, Gerald?" her stepmother demanded.

"The store. Our home. Everything."

"But that's impossible. We couldn't be . . . impoverished." Marlene Matlock's voice lowered as she grasped the severity of their situation.

"Gerald, that's not possible. We helped build this town. We are the family everyone looks to. We—"

"It's not impossible, my dear."

Hearing the tiredness in her father's voice, Silver looked up.

"We are facing ruination." He ran the palm of his right hand over his bald head. "We've spent above our income for too long."

Her stepmother's ill temper returned. "Are you saying this is *my* fault? You know we couldn't allow Silvana to be married without a proper wedding."

Gerald Matlock shook his head. "It's much more than the expense of the wedding, Marlene, and you know it. I've tried to make you understand. Business has not been good for a long while. Twin Springs isn't growing as it once did. The money from selling that piece of land was to have paid off the mortgage and our other debts. With it stolen, there's nothing left to fall back on. We are out of options."

Blinking back tears, Silver watched as her father left the parlor, his shoulders slumped.

She knew the family's financial crisis was neither because of her stepmother's spending nor because of the mercantile receipts falling off. Those things hadn't helped, but the current crisis was her fault. All her fault. Hungry for a man's affections and pressured by her stepmother to find a husband, she'd fallen for Bob Cassidy's considerable charms much too easily. Why hadn't she listened to that tiny voice of doubt?

"Whatever shall we do now?" her stepmother whispered.

Silver remained silent. She had no answer.

Her stepmother turned to look at her. "That man of yours has ruined us."

"I'm sorry, Mother."

"We're *all* sorry. Much good it will do us." She dabbed beneath her eyes with a handkerchief. "Oh, we should have known the minute he came calling on you he was up to no good. Why else would he come?"

Of course they should have known. It wasn't possible Bob Cassidy could have loved Silver. It wasn't possible he'd truly wanted to marry her. Why would he? She was no great beauty like her stepsister. She had no great fortune to inherit from her father—even before this latest disaster—and she hadn't been blessed with the usual feminine attributes used to attract a man's interests.

Yes, the Matlocks should have known Bob was up to no good.

Silver rose and left the parlor. A short while later she entered her father's office at the back of the mercantile. She'd known she would find him there, going over the record books one more time.

"Papa." She brushed her fingers across the

back of his neck before resting her hand on his shoulder. "What can I do to help?"

He raised his head to look at her, and a lump formed in her throat. He looked years older than he had only a week ago. "There's nothing any of us can do, Silver. There's no proof Mr. Cassidy is the person who stole from us. And even if there was proof, it isn't likely the authorities would be able to restore our property should they find him. It's all gone. The cash. Your stepmother's jewelry. Everything."

Silver touched the necklace beneath the collar of her dress. "I still have Great-Grandmother's locket. You could sell it."

"It would never bring enough to make a difference, my girl, but thank you for offering. I know what it means to you." He patted her hand.

"Perhaps the sheriff in Denver can find . . ." She trailed off as her father shook his head.

"I doubt it." He sighed. "Sheriff Cooper promised to do what he can, but I'm afraid it will never be enough."

"God will help us, Papa. He'll show us how to save the store and our home." She said the words with more conviction than she felt.

And if He doesn't help us, I'll find a way to do it myself.

Chapter 3

Jess Owens, the Denver bank manager, rose from his desk as Silver was shown into his office the following Monday. "Good afternoon, Miss Matlock. Won't you please be seated?"

"Thank you, Mr. Owens." She settled onto the deep leather chair and folded her hands in the lap of her gingham dress. When she spoke, she tried her best to sound confident. "Thank you for seeing me on such short notice. I arrived by stagecoach in Denver only today."

"You're traveling alone?"

"My sister and her husband live in Denver, but the purpose of my visit was to see you."

A smile curved his mouth. "I see. And what is it I can do for you, Miss Matlock?"

Silver had rehearsed what she wanted to say to the banker all the way from Twin Springs. "The First Bank and Trust holds the mortgages on my parents' home and business."

He nodded.

"Matlock Mercantile," she added.

He nodded again, still without comment.

She lifted her chin. "Our store was robbed week before last, and the money in the safe was taken—the money my father intended to use to make the final mortgage payment that is due next week."

"I see." He swiveled his chair around and rose, then walked to his office door. "John," he called to his clerk, "bring me the Matlock file. Matlock Mercantile, Twin Springs." He faced her again. "May I inquire why you are here instead of your father?"

She hesitated before answering. "My father is a proud man, Mr. Owens."

"In other words, he doesn't know you've come to see me."

Desperation overwhelmed her practiced calm as she leaned forward in her chair. "It's my fault the store was robbed."

"Your fault?" He returned to his chair behind the desk.

"Yes. The man . . . the man who robbed us was—" Oh, how hard it was to admit to a stranger. "He was my fiancé."

The bank manager's brows arched as his eyes widened, but he said nothing. His clerk entered the office and laid the requested file on the banker's desk.

"Excuse me a moment, Miss Matlock." Jess Owens slid his glasses up his nose and opened the file. Thoughtfully he studied the papers inside the folder, a frown beginning to crease his fore-ead.

"Mr. Owens." Silver gripped the edge of the

desk. “Please don’t take their home or business. My father has worked hard for everything he has. He’s poured his life into that store and into the community. If you could give him some additional time, I know he will make good on the debt.” She didn’t know anything of the kind, but she said it anyway.

“Miss Matlock, there is a legal due date on the note. The final payment was a full third of the amount borrowed. A considerable sum.” He put down the file and removed his glasses. “To overlook it wouldn’t be fair to the bank’s depositors. It’s quite a large sum of money.”

The breath caught in her chest. “How much?”

He shook his head.

She took hold of the gold locket hanging around her neck. “Would this cover the amount? That’s a real diamond, Mr. Owens. The necklace belonged to my great-grandmother, so it’s quite old.”

“I’m sorry, Miss Matlock. I cannot divulge the details of your father’s loan. I can guess that your necklace wouldn’t be worth more than 10 percent of the sum owed.”

Silver felt the color drain from her face. Her father’s debt must be at least several thousand dollars. She hadn’t dreamed it could be so much. It might as well be ten million. Tears flooded her eyes, and she blinked to keep them from falling.

The banker cleared his throat. “Perhaps I could grant a brief extension. Say, ninety days?”

"Ninety days," she repeated in a whisper, grasping at hope.

"It's the best I can do."

She drew herself up. "Thank you, Mr. Owens. We'll have the money for you in ninety days. I promise."

Silver sat with her younger stepsister in the small parlor of the Downing home, sipping a cup of tea and enjoying the quiet while her two young nephews slept.

They'd spoken of numerous things since her arrival—her brother-in-law, Dan Downing's, apprenticeship with a veterinarian, the mischief her nephew Fredrick got into since he'd begun walking, the relief her stepsister, Rose, felt now that two-month-old Harry was sleeping through the night—but they couldn't avoid discussing Silver's disastrous wedding day forever.

"How is Mother?" Rose asked. "Is she . . . is she doing any better since we left Twin Springs?"

"She's taken to her bed. I don't think she'll ever forgive me for so poorly choosing a fiancé."

"Oh, Silver."

"It's all right." She drew in a deep breath and let it out slowly. "I'm not sure I can forgive myself either."

"You couldn't have known Mr. Cassidy would . . . leave you at the altar."

"Couldn't I?" Silver wasn't so sure. When she

thought back over the weeks of their courtship, she couldn't deny there had been signs of Bob's true nature. Thoughtless comments that could sting. Flirtations with other women that he brushed off as meaningless. A seeming obsession with money. Her father's money in particular.

"Well, I'm glad you came for a visit," Rose continued. "We'll do all sorts of things to take your mind off of him while you're in Denver."

"I didn't come here to be entertained."

Rose tilted her head in silent inquiry.

"Papa could lose the store . . . and the house."

"What?"

"There are mortgages on both of them. Apparently the store hasn't been doing as well as it used to when Twin Springs was growing rapidly. Papa had that land out by Copper Creek, and he sold it, meaning to use the proceeds to pay off the notes, which are coming due. Only the money was in the safe."

"Oh no." Rose covered her mouth.

"Oh yes."

"Doesn't Sheriff Cooper hold out any hope of finding Mr. Cassidy?"

"He thinks he's long gone from the Denver area. They'll keep looking, of course, but he wasn't very encouraging. There's so little to go on, and no real evidence Bob was involved in the theft. Miss Harris—you remember the dressmaker?—swears she saw him leaving town the night before."

"Whatever will Papa do if he loses the store? And Mother. She'll never forgive—" Rose broke off suddenly.

Silver understood anyway. "I know. She'll never forgive me." She drew in a deep breath. "Before coming here this morning, I went to see the banker. He's agreed to give Papa another ninety days to raise the money."

"Will that be enough time? If Dan and I had anything extra, we would—"

Silver gave her stepsister a sad smile. "I know you would. But Dan's only an apprentice, and you have two babies to support. Father would never ask you to help. This is my fault. I'm the one who has to help recover what was taken."

That night, Silver lay sleepless in a bed in her sister and brother-in-law's home. Try as she might, she couldn't stop her racing thoughts.

This *was* her fault. She was the one who had made Bob Cassidy a part of her family, even before the wedding could take place. She was the one who'd convinced her father to give Bob—a newcomer to Twin Springs—a job in the mercantile. She was the one who had taught him all the inner workings of the business and showed him how to tally the day's receipts. It was she who had told him her father took his deposits to the bank in Denver every other week because of a long-running dispute with the Twin Springs bank manager.

Was that when Bob had decided to steal the money in the safe? Or had he made that decision only after he decided to leave her at the altar?

Her cheeks grew hot as the sting of mortification returned. She'd waited for Bob at the church for more than an hour on her wedding day—along with her father, stepmother, stepsister, brother-in-law, nephews, and all of their guests. They'd waited and waited and waited. She'd heard the whispers, seen the pity in the townspeople's eyes.

How she hated Bob for humiliating her that way. He'd played her for a fool, then compounded it by stealing from her parents. She couldn't let him get away with it. She had to find him and get back their money. She had to save her father from financial destruction.

She remembered him, then, that man who'd stood beside his horse outside the Mountain Rose Saloon. She'd been running from the church, angry and embarrassed, shamed and disgraced, hating the tears that streaked her cheeks. Then she'd looked up and there he'd stood, a stranger, tall and rugged beneath a dusty brown hat.

And he'd smirked at her!

"We going or not, bounty?"

As the words replayed in her memory, she sat up in bed. Of course. Why hadn't she thought of it before? A bounty hunter. If the sheriff hadn't enough deputies or enough cause to look for Bob Cassidy, she could hire someone to do it for her. Who better than someone who tracked down criminals for the reward?

She fingered the locket at her throat. It was all she had. It wasn't enough to pay off the mortgage, but it was surely worth enough to hire a bounty hunter. She would do so first thing tomorrow.

Chapter 4

Jared leaned back in the chair and let his gaze move over the customers in the restaurant. His mood was black, and it didn't help to think about his lack of funds. According to the sheriff, Rick Cooper, problems with the paperwork would delay collection of the reward for Lute Peterson for at least a couple more weeks, maybe longer. The waiting was driving Jared crazy. He wasn't used to staying in one place very long.

He rubbed the old wound in his shoulder. Whenever he became frustrated or angry, the pain returned, reminding him why he wasn't at home in Kentucky, reminding him why he lived the kind of life he did. It wasn't what he'd been born to. It was a life thrust upon him by the acts of an evil man, a life Jared couldn't change until he obtained justice.

With the scrape of wood against wood, he pushed back his chair, rose, and dropped the coins for his meal beside his empty plate. Then he left the restaurant and strode along the boardwalk toward the sheriff's office.

The morning air was crisp, a light wind blowing down from the snowcapped mountains to the west. But spring was coming to the mile-high city of Denver. He hoped he wouldn't be around, cooling his heels, when it arrived.

At the sheriff's office, he pushed open the door to the front entry. Through another doorway he could see Rick Cooper seated behind his desk, a woman in a blue dress standing before him, her back to Jared.

"It's a bad idea, Miss Matlock." Rick shook his head.

"But, Sheriff Cooper, you said yourself you haven't enough deputies. Why shouldn't I hire someone to do what you're unable to do?"

Her voice told Jared this Miss Matlock was young, but lack of years hadn't made her timid. She spoke with firmness, and she stood straight, her shoulders level, her head held high.

Rick continued, "The type of men who do this sort of work are more often than not hardly better than the criminals they seek."

Jared moved to the office doorway, then stopped and waited to be noticed.

The woman answered Rick. "I don't care as long as they do what they're hired to do."

Jared cleared his throat, announcing his presence. Rick leaned to the side to peer around the young woman, and Jared gave a quick nod of greeting.

Then Miss Matlock turned, and Jared found himself looking into a pair of familiar gray eyes. He would have known her anywhere. The angry bride from Twin Springs, only without tears this time. He'd thought her pretty the first time he'd seen her. Now he realized *pretty* was an inadequate description. *Striking* seemed a more appropriate word.

He knew the moment she recognized him too. Her face paled, then flushed with what he supposed was embarrassment.

Rick stood. "Morning, Newman."

"Cooper."

Something in Rick's expression changed. A slight widening of the eyes, followed by the hint of a smile. He held Jared's gaze a moment, then motioned him into the room before looking back to the woman between them.

Why did Jared have the feeling he was stepping into a well-set trap?

"Miss Matlock," the sheriff said, "may I introduce Jared Newman? He's someone I could recommend to you."

Miss Matlock had regained her composure. “How do you do, Mr. Newman.” Her tone was frosty. He supposed he couldn’t blame her, given the last time they’d seen each other.

“Pleased to make your acquaintance, miss.” He bent the brim of his hat.

Unflinching, her eyes continued to study him. All sign of her embarrassment had disappeared. No simpering female, this one. He saw grit and determination in her gaze. He found the look appealing.

“You’re a bounty hunter?” she asked.

“That’s what some call what I do.”

“Are you looking for employment?”

He glanced at Cooper, wondering how he should respond. The sheriff shrugged.

“The sheriff seems to think you could find someone for me, Mr. Newman.”

“You don’t say. And who would that be?”

Her shoulders squared. “I need you to find my . . . my fiancé.” She shook her head. “My former fiancé.”

Was this some sort of joke? Chase down the man who’d jilted her? He hadn’t been reduced to that kind of work, had he? At least with real criminals he could feel he’d accomplished something for the greater good when he turned them over to the law.

Something in his expression must have conveyed his thoughts. Her eyes narrowed. “It’s imperative I find him soon, Mr. Newman. Will you help me? I . . . I'm offering a reward."

"Miss Matlock," Rick interrupted before Jared could answer, "why don't you go back to your sister's and let me discuss the matter with Mr. Newman?"

"But I—"

"Go along, Miss Matlock. I'll be there as soon as possible."

She looked between the two men, pink rising in her cheeks for the second time since Jared's arrival. "Very well. I'll be at my sister's. You know the address."

Rick nodded.

Jared stepped to the side. Miss Matlock avoided his eyes as she moved past him. He waited until she exited to the street before speaking. "Cooper, I don't hunt down missing bridegrooms."

"There's more to it than that. Miss Matlock believes the man she was to marry stole money and jewelry from her parents before he left town. A considerable sum."

"That's adding insult to injury, but I still don't—"

"If you're looking to collect a reward, that's all I've got to offer you right now. Otherwise I guess you can wait around for the paperwork to get straightened out on Peterson."

Jared swallowed the oath rising in his throat.

"Look. You'd be helping me out. She's

determined to find this guy, and I'm afraid she might get herself into trouble if left to her own devices. She just might get robbed a second time. Or something worse."

Jared thought of his sister. Katrina had been like Miss Matlock. Not in appearance. His sister had been fair—straight blonde hair and blue eyes—while Miss Matlock had an olive complexion and curly black hair. But Katrina had had a stubborn streak a mile long. When she'd determined she wanted something, nothing had been able to stop her until she obtained it. He suspected Miss Matlock was much the same. Rick was right. She would probably get herself into trouble without his help.

"What's she offering?" he asked, fearing any attempts to refuse this job would fail, and both men knew it.

"We didn't get to that part."

Twin Springs' leading family. That's what the bartender had called the Matlocks. Reason to assume the reward could be substantial. It couldn't hurt to look into it.

"Think of it as a favor to me," the sheriff added for good measure.

Silver paced the length of the Downing parlor. Back and forth. Back and forth. Each time she arrived at the fireplace, she looked at the clock on the mantel, noting the passage of time. Two hours. It had been two hours since she'd left the sheriff's office. Why hadn't Rick Cooper come?

He just wanted to get rid of me.

She'd failed. Her beloved father would lose his store and the family home. Her stepmother would never forgive Silver. Never.

What am I to do? What am I—

A knock at the door stopped her midpace. "I'll get it, Rose," she called up the stairs. A moment later she yanked open the door, hoping beyond hope to find Sheriff Cooper standing on the front porch.

It wasn't the sheriff. It was the bounty hunter —tall and lanky, a close-trimmed mustache riding his upper lip, the shadow of a beard framing his sun-bronzed skin, a gun belt fastened low on his waist, the holsters strapped to his thigh. Jared Newman exuded confidence, power, and . . . and danger.

"The type of men who do this sort of work are more often than not hardly better than the criminals they seek."

A chill ran up her spine as she remembered the sheriff's warning.

"Miss Matlock." He bent the brim of his dusty hat. "May I speak with you?"

"Yes. I'm sorry. Yes, of course. Please come in, Mr. Newman." She stepped back, opening the door wide.

He moved inside.

The breath caught in her chest as he turned on his heel to face her again. There was something disconcerting about the way he looked at her. As if he could read her thoughts. And although he couldn't be more than a half dozen years older than she, his penetrating gaze seemed ancient, as if it had seen all the troubles of the world firsthand.

"The type of men who do this sort of work are more often than not hardly better than the criminals they seek."

He swept the hat from his head. "So, you want to find your fiancé."

"Yes."

"Still want to marry him?"

"No."

A smile crossed his mouth. There and then gone.

It wasn't the first time he'd found humor in her distress, and her dislike of him returned. She wished she could send him on his way. But she couldn't. For now, he was her only hope. "Bob Cassidy's a thief, and I want back what he took from my parents."

"The sheriff tells me there's no arrest warrant for him."

Wringing her hands, Silver walked into the parlor. "We have no proof it was Bob who broke into the safe. There's conflicting information about when he left Twin Springs." She spun around. "But I *know* he did it."

"And you're offering a reward."

"For the return of our property, yes. I want to see Bob brought to justice."

He lifted an eyebrow. "How much of a reward?"

"A hundred dollars." To Silver, the amount was a veritable fortune. But if Jared Newman was able to return the money and jewelry that had been stolen, it would be worth every penny.

He didn't react to the offer in the slightest. He simply watched her with that intense gaze of his.

"And three dollars a day up to . . . up to thirty days," she added quickly, fearing he would refuse. "To cover your expenses." If her math was correct, that would be almost another hundred dollars. Was it too much to offer? Should she take it back? Offer him less?

Still he said nothing.

Please, God. Make him agree to help me.

A hundred dollars wasn't a large reward, but if Jared found the missing fiancé within the next couple of weeks, it would be a good use of his time while he waited for the Peterson reward. And those two sums put together meant he wouldn't have to take on another job until fall, maybe even winter. And that would leave him free to focus on his personal quest for justice. Or should he call it *retribution?*

"I'll need a cash advance to buy supplies," he said at last, "and I'll need all of the information you can give me about the man you seek. Known associates. Occupation. Family. How long he lived in Twin Springs. Where he might have gone when he left. A photograph if you've got one. That sort of thing."

"Of course. But you needn't buy supplies. My parents own the mercantile in Twin Springs. They can provide whatever you need."

He shrugged his agreement. It was okay with him if she wanted to pay three dollars a day for expenses but put up the supplies as well. It would leave more money in his pocket. "Fine. Let's meet at the mercantile on Thursday morning. Say ten o'clock. You can answer all my questions then."

Relief covered her face. "Thank you, Mr. Newman. I'm forever grateful."

Chapter 5

Silver awakened on Thursday morning in her own bedroom. Not that she felt rested. She'd had a horrible argument with her stepmother the previous day after her return to Twin Springs, and the fight had invaded her dreams.

"Hiring a bounty hunter! What were you

thinking? Your reputation is already in tatters. Why must you be so foolish, Silvana?"

The words had stung then. They still stung in the morning light. She could do nothing right in her stepmother's eyes. It had always been that way, no matter how hard she'd tried to win her approval. Silver wasn't socially adept like her younger stepsister. Rose never failed to know the right thing to say or do in any given situation. She was always a lady, always impeccably groomed, never short-tempered. And from the time she was a child, Rose had instinctively known how to charm men and boys alike.

Silver was the exact opposite—especially when it came to men.

She covered her eyes with the crook of her arm, remembering a steady progression of mistakes she'd made in the company of the stronger sex, especially when it came to voicing her opinions without any invitation to do so. It hadn't been until Bob Cassidy came to Twin Springs, six months prior, that Silver even cared she wasn't beautiful or accomplished like her stepsister. But Bob had been a determined suitor. He hadn't seemed to mind she would rather ride her horse astride than sit in the parlor doing needlepoint. With unbelievable ease, he'd swept Silver off her feet.

But, as it turned out, it wasn't Silver he'd wanted. She'd merely been the way to her father's safe. She shouldn't be surprised. It shouldn't hurt so much. But she was and it did.

With a sigh, she shoved aside her blankets. She performed her morning ablutions with haste. As for her unruly hair, she captured it with a ribbon at the nape. That would have to do.

When she entered the kitchen a short while later, she found her stepmother seated at the table, sipping coffee from a china cup. Her father stood near the stove, scrambling eggs in a skillet.

"Good morning, Mother. Father."

"Good morning, Silver." Her father tossed a smile over his shoulder.

Her stepmother was silent, and her expression said she was still angry.

Silver stopped next to her father and poured herself a cup of coffee from the pot on the stove.

"One or two eggs, honey?"

She met her father's gaze. "Nothing for me. Thanks, Papa." She turned to lean her backside against the worktable. "I'm going over to the store right away to put together the supplies for Mr. Newman. I want him to begin his search as soon as possible."

Her stepmother set down her cup with a clatter. "Gerald, Silver should have nothing further to do with that . . . that man. It isn't proper for her to do so. If he must search for Mr. Cassidy, then let him deal directly with you or the sheriff."

"Mother, Sheriff Cooper wouldn't have recommended Mr. Newman if he wasn't a reputable man." Silver wasn't certain she spoke the truth, but her parents needn't know that.

Her stepmother stood. "I don't know why I waste my breath trying to protect and guide you. You always do as you wish anyway. I've done my best for you. I truly have. Why must you be so foolish and headstrong? There's nothing we can do about your being jilted, but your behavior after the fact? It's unacceptable! Why can't you be more like Rose?" With a disappointed huff, she swept out of the kitchen.

Her father patted her shoulder. "She doesn't mean to hurt you."

She may not mean to, but she does, all the time. Silver gave him a brief smile before pressing her cheek against his chest, words unnecessary between them.

She'd always been her papa's girl, and she adored him in return. She didn't disappoint him the way she did her stepmother. He didn't expect her to conform. He'd never pressured her to find a husband or to dress a certain way or to speak differently. He simply loved her.

Silver drew back and kissed her father on the cheek. "I'd better get over to the store."

"Go ahead. Your mother and I will be there soon."

The morning air was cool, causing Silver to draw her shawl closer around her shoulders as she hurried to the mercantile. She let herself in the back door and from the pocket of her dress pulled the slip of paper on which Jared Newman had scrawled a list of supplies. Flour. Salted beef. Dried fruit. Cornmeal. Coffee. Sugar. Soda. Salt. Lard. Beans. Oats. Barley. Rice. And more. Foodstuffs meant to keep a body alive rather than to satisfy a discriminating palate. Two weeks' worth, he'd told her.

Could the bounty hunter find Bob in that amount of time? He had to. He must. Her erstwhile fiancé had left Twin Springs eleven days earlier. Would he still have the money and jewels he'd stolen? It might already be too late. Bob could have spent it or lost it in less time than that.

Panic washed over her. Jared Newman had to find Bob, and Bob had to have their money. There was so little time to rescue her family.

I should go with Mr. Newman.

The idea quickened her pulse. It would be so much better than sitting here waiting, doing nothing, feeling helpless, listening to her step-mother's complaints. She knew Bob. Maybe not as well as she'd thought she did, but certainly better than Jared Newman. All the bounty hunter would have was a crinkled photograph and whatever Silver told him. But if she went with Mr. Newman, she could increase the chances Bob would be found.

No, she couldn't do it. An unmarried woman of twenty-one years traveling unescorted with a man would set every gossip's tongue wagging from Twin Springs all the way to Denver. It didn't matter that she could ride as well as any man or that she could fire a pistol and hit a target with some accuracy. It didn't matter that she'd often slept under the stars as a child when she and her father had gone fishing. None of it mattered. It would still be considered scandalous. Whatever good reputation she had left would be destroyed. She couldn't go. Her father would never allow it. Her stepmother already thought her unredeem-able.

Papa and Mother don't have to know. I don't have to tell them.

But she couldn't. She really couldn't do it. No matter how much she wished she could.

Unlike the last time Jared was through Twin Springs, the town didn't look deserted this morning. Three men stood deep in conversation outside the bank. Up ahead two women carrying baskets entered the mercantile. A wagon pulled by a team of horses stood outside the feed store, where several customers were visible through the large front window. Piano music drifted through the swinging doors of the Mountain Rose Saloon.

Jared reined in at the Matlock Mercantile. The

store had the same false-front facade as the other buildings on the town's main street, but this one was freshly whitewashed, the store's name painted in wide black letters above the awning. He dismounted, spurs jingling. With a quick flip of his wrist, he wrapped the reins around the hitching rail, then stepped onto the boardwalk. Pausing, he perused his surroundings one more time before entering the store.

The interior of Matlock Mercantile was similar to stores in every town Jared had been in from Kentucky to Texas to Wyoming. Every spare inch was designed to hold merchandise. Display tables held fabric, cooking utensils, lamps, and other sundry items. Glass cases revealed sharp knives and a few pieces of jewelry. Dry goods and foodstuffs filled the shelves lining the walls from floor to ceiling.

The two women who'd entered the mercantile a few minutes before Jared were looking at bolts of cloth on a table nearest the door. They glanced in his direction, then dropped their gazes. One leaned closer to the other and whispered, "That must be him. The bounty hunter."

It appeared the local gossips had heard he was coming. Not that he was surprised by it or cared what they said. He'd learned that a man who spent his life chasing down criminals for the rewards offered wasn't highly esteemed. Not even by most of the people he served. But he hadn't chosen this profession, if it could be called that. It had been thrust upon him by circum-tances. Still, the work served its purpose. Delivering fugitives from the law to jail gave Jared the ability to continue the search that mattered most to him. Who was he to argue with fate? Certainly he wouldn't be dissuaded by those who gossiped about him.

A voice from long ago whispered in his memory. His mother's, speaking to his sister. *"Tattlers and busybodies speak things which they ought not. Never become one of them, Katrina. Guard your lips and mind."*

Katrina. Precious Katrina. His sister had had the purest of hearts, along with the strongest of wills. And his beloved mother and father had been the finest people he'd known. Six years hadn't lessened how much he missed the family that had been taken from him.

He gave his head a quick shake, throwing off painful memories as he strode down the aisle toward the counter. Just before he arrived, Silver Matlock appeared in the doorway to a back room. An expression of relief crossed her face the instant she saw him. Had she doubted he would show up? Probably. But she had good reason to doubt a man's word after what had happened to her.

"Miss Matlock." He tugged the brim of his hat.

"Mr. Newman."

"Have you got the supplies ready?"

She nodded. "Yes. Everything is over there." She pointed to the far end of the counter.

From the looks of it, she hadn't held back anything he'd requested. "How about the information I asked for?"

"I wrote it all down for you. Everything I know." She glanced toward the fabric table—and the two whispering customers—at the front of the store. "Why don't you come into the back room where we can talk privately?"

So he was right about those young women. Gossips. And they hadn't whispered only about the bounty hunter who'd ridden into town. He had the feeling—judging by Silver's expression—that they'd been gossiping about her too.

Without a word he followed Silver through the back storage room and into a cluttered office.

She moved to the opposite side of the desk before facing him again. "Everything's here. There's a photograph. It's the only one I have. And a description of Bob, his habits, his work . . ." A blush rose in her cheeks. "Some of the information isn't as detailed as I would like. I . . . I'm afraid I didn't know him as well as I thought. It was a whirlwind romance, and at the time I thought him utterly charming. But perhaps everything he told me about himself was a lie."

Jared took the slip of paper and photograph from atop the desk. She'd told the truth about what she'd written down. It wasn't a detailed accounting. "This isn't much to go on, Miss Matlock. Your description could fit a dozen men in this town alone."

"There wasn't much more to say," she answered softly.

He touched the paper with his index finger. "You mention here something about a man in Central City. A Mr. Carlton."

"Yes. Bob knew someone named Carlton who was a dealer in one of the gaming halls there, but Carlton could be his first name or his last. I'm not sure. Bob mentioned him in passing when we were planning the ceremony. I thought he meant to invite him to the wedding."

"No family anywhere?"

She shook her head. "He told me he had a half brother, but I think the brother must be dead. Bob didn't seem to want to talk about him. I know his parents are deceased. They died during the war."

"He wasn't from Twin Springs?"

"No. He arrived here about six months ago. He lived in Missouri before he came to Colorado."

"Then I guess I'll start my search in Central City for his friend." He folded the paper in half, then again. "You said this was your only photograph of Mr. Cassidy. It's not very good."

"I know. Bob didn't like to have his picture taken." The color in her cheeks deepened. "We were supposed to have one taken on our wedding day. Together."

He caught the glitter of tears in her eyes before she looked away, and he felt an unexpected wish to comfort her. But in the next instant she lifted her chin, holding herself erect, her stance proud and determined.

Whatever else Cassidy is, he's an idiot for leaving her. The thought was even more unexpected—not to mention unwelcome—than the wish to comfort her.

Jared cleared his throat as he shoved the paper and photograph into the pocket of his shirt. "I'd best get those supplies loaded on my pack-horse. I'd like to make Central City by tomorrow night."

"Please wait a moment. My father wants to speak with you."

"Fair enough."

Half an hour later, Silver stood at the window in the front of the store, watching Jared Newman ride down Main Street astride his black-and-white pinto. Following behind was a sorrel packhorse, laden with supplies.

Please, God. Let him find Bob before it's too late.

She turned around. Hazel Rathdrum and her sister, Celeste, were still in the store, only now they were at the counter, paying Silver's stepmother for their purchases. They were talking, but their voices were too low for Silver to make out what was said. From the pained expression on her stepmother's face, she suspected it was about her. How could they not talk about her? Being jilted in such a public fashion wasn't something that happened every day in their small town. Being jilted by a suspected thief was an even worse offense. And now she'd hired a bounty hunter. Scandalous! This could keep them talking for weeks.

Silver straightened her shoulders. What did she care what those two busybodies said? At least Bob had abandoned her before the wedding. It would have been a far worse fate to be married to a thief and a liar. Her family should thank God for saving her from that end.

Holding her head high, she walked down the aisle and stepped behind the counter, stopping beside her stepmother.

Hazel looked at her with concerned eyes. "How are you, Miss Matlock?"

"I'm well, thank you, Miss Rathdrum."

"How was your visit with your dear stepsister?" Celeste chimed in.

"We had a lovely visit. I adore my nephews."

Hazel leaned forward, as if about to share an intimate secret. "Was that him? Was that the man you hired to find Mr. Cassidy?"

Silver felt her stepmother stiffen.

Celeste said, "Wherever did you find a bounty hunter?"

Her stepmother whispered an apology and retreated through the doorway to the back room before Silver could answer the question.

Hazel glanced at her sister. "There was something rather frightening about him, don't you think?" Her gaze returned to Silver. "Gracious. I don't know where you get the courage to do some of the things you do. Going to Denver without a chaperone. Hiring a gunfighter."

"Mr. Newman isn't a gunfighter. He tracks down people who are running from the law. The sheriff himself recommended him to me." She forced a smile. "Is there anything else I can help you with, Miss Rathdrum? I wouldn't want to keep you if you've finished with your shopping." Her invitation for the pair of young women to leave was as obvious as she could make it without actually saying the words.

Hazel understood. "Come along, Celeste." With a huff, she turned and hooked arms with her sister. Then the two of them left the store.

Good riddance.

Silver never had liked those two. The Rathdrum sisters were mean-spirited. Much like scavengers in the animal kingdom, they liked to attack the weakest, the easy prey. Now they thought Silver was vulnerable. Perhaps so, but she wasn't going to lie there and take it. She wouldn't allow her present or her future to be defined by the mistake of succumbing to Bob Cassidy's charms.

Drawing in a determined breath, she turned and followed the sound of her parents' voices to the office.

"She must go," her stepmother said as Silver entered the room. "Silvana must go at once. Today."

Her father glanced toward the doorway.

Silver stopped. "Where must I go today?"

"Your mother wishes for you to return to your sister's."

"For how long?"

"Until the talk dies down," her stepmother answered without looking at her.

"Gossip doesn't bother me." The lie tasted metallic on her tongue. It did bother her, but it would bother her more to be sent away in disgrace. It seemed so . . . so cowardly. It made her feel even more of a disappointment and failure.

Her stepmother drew herself up, her hands folded before her waist. "I don't want to argue with you, Silvana Matlock. Go to your room and pack your things. You will leave for Denver on the afternoon stage. We shall brook no argument from you this time. You will not shame your family's good name any further."

Chapter 6

Jared made camp as dusk settled over the earth, shadows long and the temperature already falling. It promised to be a cold night. He was thankful for the fire and for the windbreak provided by a wall of rocks about fifteen or twenty yards from the road.

He'd finished eating his supper when he heard something, a sound that didn't belong with the night. The hair on the back of his neck rose. At the same moment he got to his feet, he saw the horses lift their heads and look toward the west. He stepped away from the fire, his right hand hovering above his gun.

"Mr. Newman?"

The sound of a woman's voice was the last thing he'd expected.

"Is that you, Mr. Newman?" Silver Matlock moved into the firelight, leading a horse behind her.

He should have been surprised to see her, but he wasn't. Not really. He lowered his hand to his side. "What are you doing here, Miss Matlock?" He didn't have to ask how she'd found him. There was only one road leading from Twin Springs up to Central City, and his campfire would have been easy to see, even for an untrained eye.

“I . . . I’ve decided to join you.”

Now he was surprised. “You what?”

She lifted her chin in a show of determination, squinting into the shadows where he stood. “I’ve decided to go with you to find Bob.”

Was she joking? “No, you’re not. That wasn’t part of our agreement.”

“It’s something I must do.”

Jared stepped closer to the fire, allowing her to see more than his shadow.

“Please, Mr. Newman. You said yourself the photograph isn’t very good and my description could fit a lot of other men. But I’ll know Bob when I see him. If I’m along, you won’t overlook him by accident. Besides, I . . . I can’t stay behind. I need to help. I must do something or I’ll go crazy.”

Jared knew when someone wasn’t telling the whole truth. The years had taught him to read people. Without a doubt, Silver Matlock was holding something back.

“Surely, Mr. Newman, two of us looking for Bob would be better than one.”

“Maybe. Maybe not. You’d probably be in my way. Besides, I can’t believe your parents would agree to this.”

“You’re wrong. They would rather I went elsewhere. At least my stepmother would. She wants me anywhere else than in Twin Springs. I’m an embarrassment to her. She cannot bear the gossip.”

Jared knew what a person said aloud had to be weighed along with facial expression, the tone of voice, even body movement. And what he saw when he looked at Silver was a wounded spirit. He was convinced that was due less to Bob Cassidy's jilting of her than to her stepmother's acid tongue. Mrs. Matlock had directed several cutting remarks at her daughter within Jared's hearing before he'd ridden out of Twin Springs.

He cleared his throat. "Coming with me would expose you to even more gossip. Your father seems a caring man. He wouldn't want more hurt heaped upon you."

"My father *is* caring, but he usually does whatever my stepmother wishes in order to keep peace in our home. And for the present, she wants me gone."

The desperation and heartache in her eyes weakened his resolve.

"Please." She took a step closer to the fire. "I need to do this, Mr. Newman. I can't go back. I can't be shut away in shame while my father loses all he's worked for."

He tried to harden himself against her desperate plea. "This isn't a Sunday ride in the country I'm going on, Miss Matlock. I'll be moving hard and fast, and you won't find much comfort on the trail."

"I'm not a hothouse flower, sir. I can take it if you can."

"You don't have the faintest notion what you'd be getting yourself into."

"I know it won't be easy, but I'm strong. I won't hinder you. I swear to you, I won't."

He raked the fingers of his left hand through his hair, more irritated with himself than with her. Because he should be able to send her away without even a tiny twinge of conscience or remorse. He should, but he couldn't seem to do it. "All right, Miss Matlock. Can't do anything about it tonight anyway. You can go with me as far as Central City, and we'll have to see after that. But if you give me any trouble, I'll send you packing in a heartbeat. Understood?"

"Understood." A faint smile whispered across her lips. "I won't be any trouble. I promise."

He wasn't fool enough to believe that was the truth.

Silver lay with her back to the fire, listening to the sounds of the night. One of the horses stomped a foot at regular intervals. A breeze rustled the tall pine trees nearby. An owl hooted in the distance. And softer than all the other sounds—and yet somehow more resounding in her ears—she heard Jared Newman's slow and steady breathing from where he lay on the other side of the campfire.

She shouldn't have said her father did whatever his wife told him. While it was mostly the truth, it painted her father in an unfair light. He was a good and decent man. Just not strong when it came to standing up to his second wife's iron will.

Silver also shouldn't have said her parents wouldn't care where she went. Her father would care. He would worry. And to be fair, her stepmother would worry too.

However, her parents *had* sent her away. They'd sent her to Denver, her buckskin mare tied to the back of the stagecoach. But before the stage traveled far, Silver had insisted the driver stop so she could get off. She'd had to. She couldn't be sent to stay with her stepsister. Doing nothing would have driven her mad. Better to be here, with this bounty hunter, helping to find Bob, helping to rescue her family from the looming financial disaster, than sitting around feeling guilty.

She rolled onto her back and stared through the tree limbs at the star-spattered sky, the moon having passed beyond the mountains in the west.

Unwelcomed, the recollection of another night when the stars had ruled the heavens entered her thoughts. The night Bob had kissed her for the first time. The night he'd asked her to marry him. She remembered the swirl of emotions sweeping through her. Had any of those emotions been love? No, she thought not. At least not the romantic kind as portrayed in novels and poetry.

Not the kind of love Rose felt for her husband. But Silver had thought her affection for Bob—and his for her—would be enough to build a marriage on, and so she'd accepted his proposal, not knowing how deeply she would come to regret it.

She had only one chance to make it right. And she was taking it.

Chapter 7

Jared Newman wasn't much of a talker. He hadn't said a single word to Silver since they'd broken camp a half hour after sunrise. She was fine with the silence. After a mostly sleepless night, her brain felt foggy, and she doubted she could engage in conversation, intelligent or otherwise.

Following behind the pinto and packhorse, she found her gaze focused on the bounty hunter's back. He rode with the ease of a man who'd spent a great deal of time in the saddle. His body flowed with the horse's movements, his right hand resting on his thigh. She suspected that, despite looking relaxed, he was alert for signs of danger.

Danger must be a constant part of his life.

How had he become a bounty hunter? There was something about him—something more than just the soft southern drawl—that told her he'd been raised in a much different world from the one he lived in now. A gentleman's world. Something in his eyes, perhaps. Or something in the way he . . .

She shook off the train of thought. It didn't matter to her, one way or another, where he'd come from or who he'd once been.

As the trail widened, Jared slowed his gelding and waited for Silver to come alongside him. "You know, Miss Matlock, Central City is a shot in the dark. Your Mr. Cassidy might not have come to see his friend before leaving Colorado. He could be anywhere by now."

"I know."

"If his friend is a professional gambler, he'll be working in one of the saloons. You won't be able to go with me while I look for him."

She didn't like it, but she didn't argue with him. She'd never been inside a saloon in her life. Although it couldn't damage her reputation any more than traveling alone with this man might do.

"There's a restaurant in Central City that's reputable. I ate there last time I came through these parts. I'll have you wait for me there. Remember what I told you last night. If you don't do as I say, I'll send you packing."

The repeated warning caused Silver's temper to rise, but she tamped it down. She'd set herself on this course and was determined to see it through. No matter what, she wouldn't give Jared Newman a reason to send her back to Twin Springs.

"Agreed, Miss Matlock?"

"Agreed, Mr. Newman. I promise you, I'll adhere to your rules."

His gaze told her she'd best keep that promise. Then he nudged his horse with his heels and pulled out in front of her once again.

Black Hawk—and Central City above it—was a town built in a narrow draw between mountains rich with ore. While the gold rush days were over, the mines would, it was believed, produce wealth for decades to come. At least for a fortunate few.

It was early afternoon when Jared and Silver rode through Black Hawk on their way to Central City. Music and laughter spilled from several saloons lining the main street. Jared paid close attention to each establishment that provided games of chance for its customers. If he'd been alone, he would have dismounted and begun his search right then. But he wasn't alone, which meant he had to see Silver settled someplace he considered safe.

What a bother. And it was his own fault for agreeing she could go with him, even for one day. A man in his profession needed to be untethered by responsibilities. That was why he worked alone. Always had. Always would.

They rode on to Central City and to the restaurant he'd mentioned earlier. After tying their horses to the hitching rail, he led the way inside, where a waitress in a white blouse and black skirt showed them to a table beside the front window. Silver sat on one of the chairs, then looked at him with a question in her eyes.

"I'll be back as soon as I can," he told her. "You stay put." He put several coins on the table in front of her. "Get yourself something to eat. With any luck, we'll be on our way in an hour or two."

"Aren't you going to eat?"

"Not right now." He started to turn, then repeated, "Stay put."

From the look Silver gave him, he could tell she wanted to argue with him. Her expressive eyes always gave away her true feelings. But to her credit, she nodded in agreement and said nothing more.

He left the restaurant and walked to the nearest saloon. Inside, smoke formed a cloud above the two tables where men played cards. Several women were scattered around the open-spaced room, two lounging against the bar, three others seated at the card tables with the players. The tinkle and bang of a piano sounded from a far corner.

Jared strode to the bar, and when the man behind it asked what he wanted, he answered, "Information."

The bartender cocked an eyebrow.

"I'm looking for a gambler by the name of Carlton. A dealer. I was told he works in Central City. Do you know him?"

"Sorry. Can't say as I do. You a lawman?"

Jared gave a slow shake of his head. "I was asked to pass along a message about a family friend if I happened to run into him while in town." The lie came easily to his lips. Subterfuge and deception were a necessary part of tracking down fugitives. It no longer bothered him when the situation called for less than truthful answers, although occasionally he wondered what his mother and father would think if they could see what he'd become.

The bartender took a glass from behind the counter and wiped it with a towel. "Try the Crystal Palace." He jerked his head to the left. "They've got a dozen or so dealers on their payroll. Might be the guy you're lookin' for is one of them."

"Thanks." Jared touched the brim of his hat. "I'll do that."

A short while later, he leaned against another bar, this one inside the Crystal Palace. The large room held few similarities with most saloons that lined the streets of mining towns. Somebody had spent a lot of money so the place could live up to its name. Crystal chandeliers hung from the ceiling. Red velvet curtains framed the large windows. Leather-upholstered wing chairs were grouped together as if this were a gentlemen's club rather than a gambling establishment.

Although it was not even suppertime, the green felt tables had plenty of men seated at them. Smoke from their cigarettes and cigars curled toward the high ceilings. The women who worked in the Crystal Palace were clad in satin gowns. Their makeup was discreet, their hair perfectly coiffed. One could almost believe they were ladies of quality, the sort who used to attend balls at Fair Acres as guests of his parents.

But Jared was not deceived by appearances. He could tell the difference between a harlot and a lady. His mother had been a true lady, a woman of character, full of charity and kindness. There'd been an innocence about her too, despite the hardships endured during the war.

Come to think of it, he'd recognized that same strength of character in Silver Matlock. She was both fragile and tough, determined and uncertain, innocent and wise. Those were just a few of the reasons it was so hard for him to say no to her.

There was nothing innocent about the women in the Crystal Palace. Despite their refined appearance, he saw other things in their eyes—cynicism, pain, bitterness, greed, hate, avarice.

"Excuse me, sir. There's an opening at the tables if you're interested in playing cards."

He turned toward the silken voice.

The woman's fire-red hair was caught in a mass of curls atop her head, and her green eyes looked up at him while a friendly smile played across her rosy mouth. "If you would rather, we could sit at a table and talk."

"I'd rather talk than lose money."

Her smile broadened before she turned, the hem of her gown sweeping the shiny black-and-white tiled floor, and led the way to a table in a more private corner of the room. She waited beside a chair until Jared pulled it out for her.

"You're not from around here," she said as she sat. "I would remember you if you'd been in before."

He shook his head. "No, miss. I'm not from around here."

"My name is Claudette."

He dipped his head. "Pleased to make your acquaintance. You can call me Jared."

"What brings you to Central City? Are you hoping to strike it rich?"

He laughed softly. "I'm not that big of a fool. Actually, I'm looking for someone. There's a member of his family who needs to find him, and I promised to help. His name's Bob Cassidy. I just missed him awhile back in Twin Springs, but I heard he was coming up this way to see a friend named Carlton. Do you know anybody by that name?"

Claudette smiled. "Matt Carlton? Sure, I know him. He used to work here as a dealer. But he up and quit last week. Or maybe it was before that. Anyway, one day he was here and the next he was gone. That's how it is with lots of folks hereabouts."

Was Carlton's departure a coincidence? Jared didn't tend to believe in coincidence. The two friends, Carlton and Cassidy, must have joined forces. "Did he leave with Mr. Cassidy, by any chance?"

"Sorry." She shook her head. "Don't know."

"Could you describe this Carlton fellow to me? Might make it easier for me to find the two of them. It's important."

"Sure I can. Matt's a tall man. Got dark yellow hair and pale blue eyes. Handsome devil, if you ask me, but I never took to him. Had a cold way about him."

Jared leaned forward on his chair. "By chance did he leave word where he was going?"

"No. Like I said, he was here one day and gone the next. But he was always talking about making it rich in one mining camp or another. Montana. Idaho. Nevada." She shrugged. "Anyplace he could sit at a poker table and take some poor sucker's hard-earned dust."

Jared had known it was a long shot he would find Bob Cassidy in Central City with his friend. But wouldn't it have been nice to collect the reward after only two days? He'd have been rid of Silver Matlock too.

He pushed his chair back a few inches, preparing to rise. "Thank you for your help, Miss Claudette. I guess I'll—"

"Claudette." The pretty brunette who'd interrupted leaned close to Claudette's ear. "You're needed upstairs. It's Felicity."

The woman was instantly on her feet. "You must excuse me." With that, she hurried toward the curving staircase that led to the second floor, the brunette following on her heels.

Jared rose and returned to the bar.

"Want another?" the bartender asked.

He shook his head. "No, thanks. What's wrong with Felicity?"

The bartender's jaw tightened. "Some man beat her to within an inch of her life. Unconscious for days. The doctor says she'll likely pull through, but it won't be easy and she won't ever be the same."

Jared had asked the question as a way to strike up another conversation, hoping the information he'd sought from Claudette could now be obtained from the bartender instead.

"Beat her so bad she doesn't hardly have a face left. Chopped off her hair too."

Icy fingers closed around Jared's heart. He forgot about the man named Matt Carlton who'd been a dealer in this establishment. He forgot about the thieving Bob Cassidy who'd left his bride at the altar after emptying the mercantile safe. He forgot everything except for the last words the barkeeper had spoken: *"Chopped off her hair too."*

It had been over a year since he'd tracked the killer with the crescent scar to Colorado. Over a year since he'd heard of another murder. Jared had used the time to bring in other fugitives, but he was ever vigilant for a new clue—or another tragedy. It seemed he had stumbled onto the latter today.

He spun away from the bar and strode toward the staircase.

Chapter 8

Silver couldn't sit still any longer. She'd eaten her early dinner and consumed too many cups of coffee while waiting for Jared to return to the restaurant. The afternoon shadows had grown long. Dusk would soon arrive.

Glancing out the window, she confirmed that all three horses were still tethered to the rail beyond the glass. Good. It meant the bounty hunter hadn't abandoned her. But he had left her there a long while, and if she didn't get a bit of fresh air, she would explode with frustration. Jared Newman had told her to stay put. He'd warned her what would happen if she disobeyed him, promising to send her back to her parents if she caused him any trouble. But surely he couldn't object to her waiting with the horses.

After paying for her meal, she went outside, pausing on the boardwalk to look up and down the street. Many more horses were tied at the rails outside the numerous saloons. Many more men stood and walked on the boardwalks too. Boisterous and loud men.

She stepped into the street and moved to stand near her mare's head. Stroking the horse's muzzle, she said, "Cinder, do you suppose he's learned anything about Bob?"

The buckskin snorted and bobbed her head.

Silver laughed softly. "I wish I could be as optimistic as you." Then she pressed her forehead against the mare's neck. "Please, God. Let Mr. Newman find Bob and all that he stole. Help me restore what was taken from my father. None of this was his fault. Father shouldn't be punished for my poor judgment."

Tears sprang to her eyes, and her throat tightened. Perhaps if she'd asked the Lord if she should marry Bob, she might have saved herself and her family this grief. Surely God would have warned her of her fiancé's true character.

Only You did warn me, didn't You? I just wouldn't listen.

Heaven help her. It wasn't that she didn't try

to do the right thing, but her impetuous, headstrong nature too often overruled common sense. She spoke her feelings aloud when she should keep silent. She challenged the way things were, believing she could make them what they ought to be by sheer determination. She thought herself as worthy as any man, despite society's mores that told her otherwise. Her mind was filled with ideas, the kind women of good character and respectable families weren't supposed to have.

Bob Cassidy had seemed to like those traits in her. He'd seemed to appreciate and approve of them. What an actor he'd been. What a liar.

She sniffed as she straightened away from her horse, then wiped her tears with her fingertips. She mustn't let the bounty hunter find her crying. Jared Newman was looking for any excuse to send her home, and she mustn't give him one.

It wasn't easy for Jared to convince the protective Claudette to let him talk to Felicity. But when he told her he was searching for a man who'd done to others what had been done to this girl, the woman relented.

He leaned forward on the chair next to the bed. Felicity might have been a pretty girl at one time, but it was hard to tell beneath the ugly bruises that marred her face. "My name is Jared Newman. I want to find the man who did this to you. It's possible he's done it before, and I want to bring him to justice. Can you tell me about him, miss? Anything you can remember might help me."

Felicity could open only her left eye. Her right was swollen shut. But he saw the stark fear in the other one. Would she ever again be able to look at a man without terror icing her veins? He hoped she could.

"It's all right, honey," Claudette said. "Mr. Newman wants to help. Not sure why, but I think he can be trusted."

Jared forced himself to speak in a soft, calm voice. "Can you tell me what he looked like?"

"I . . . couldn't see . . . him good. It was dark and . . . and he wore something over his face."

Jared glanced toward Claudette.

"She was attacked on her way home. Felicity doesn't live at the Crystal Palace. She and her little boy have a place of their—"

"Scar . . . ," the younger woman whispered. "He . . . had a scar."

Jared's gut tightened. Although he was certain what the answer would be, he asked anyway. "What kind of scar? What did it look like? Where was it?"

"Above his . . . collarbone." Felicity swallowed. "Here." She touched the spot at the base of her throat. "It was shaped like . . . like a half . . . moon."

It *was* him. He was here in Central City—or had been when this young woman was assaulted more than a week ago.

When he looked at Felicity again, he no longer saw her. He saw his sister. He saw Katrina's swollen face and battered body as she'd told him of her assailant's scar on his chest. That was the last thing she'd said to him before she died.

"Mr. Newman?" Claudette said, intruding on the dark memory. "I think you'd better leave now."

"Just a few more questions."

"No. Felicity's not strong enough. Please go now."

Jared wasn't going to change the woman's mind. He could tell that by the set of her mouth and the look in her eyes. As he got to his feet he said, "I'd like to come back in the morning, if that's all right. To see if there's anything else she remembers."

Claudette led him out of the room before answering. "I'm not convinced she can tell you anything more that would help. The sheriff said there was too little to go on. Not that he cares about a girl like Felicity. Still, if the law can't find him, why do you think you can?"

"Because I've been looking for him for six years, and I won't give up until I find him." The rage that filled him was a familiar companion. "He did the same thing to my sister." He drew a deep breath. "Only she didn't survive. My sister died from the assault."

Claudette's expression changed to one of sympathy. "I'm sorry to know it. If Felicity is stronger in the morning, I reckon you may see her."

"Thanks."

"Where are you staying?"

"I don't have a room yet."

"The Colorado is a decent hotel."

"Thanks. I'll go there."

"Mr. Newman, the sheriff said it isn't likely the man who did this is still in Central City. Drifters and gunslingers pass through the gold camps all the time. And I remain doubtful there's anything helpful Felicity can tell you about the man who attacked her."

"I know, Miss Claudette, but you never can tell what someone will remember that can help. Even something small." He put his hat on his head. "Let me know when I can come back in the morning."

"I will. Good night, Mr. Newman."

Despite the gray light of early evening, Silver recognized Jared as he strode along the boardwalk toward the restaurant. It was more than his height or the breadth of his shoulders. There was something in the way he moved that was already familiar to her. A strength. A sense of purpose.

Odd, wasn't it? That she should know that about him after so short a time.

Before Jared reached the restaurant doorway, Silver stepped away from the horses and into the pale light spilling onto the boardwalk through the restaurant's window. "Did you find Mr. Carlton?"

"No." He frowned. "I thought I told you to wait inside."

She straightened her shoulders, standing tall. "I sat there as long as I could, but I needed to stretch my legs. I was waiting with the horses."

"This isn't a safe town. Not for a woman alone."

"Perhaps not, but I'm unharmed. You can see that for yourself." She wished she could read his face better. "What did you learn? Anything that will help us?"

At last he too stepped into the lantern light coming from the restaurant. "I confirmed that a man named Matt Carlton used to work as a dealer at a place called the Crystal Palace." He jerked his head, indicating it was somewhere behind him. "But he quit and left town about a week or so ago. No one knows where he went for sure. Just that he talked about heading farther west."

The strength that had kept her shoulders straight drained out of her. She'd hoped—

"I'll take you back to Twin Springs in the morning, Miss Matlock."

"Take me back?" She stared at him. "After spending one afternoon in one town?"

"It's more than—"

"I haven't given you reason to go back on your word. You agreed to find Bob, and you agreed to take me with you as long as I gave you no trouble. Which I haven't, have I?"

"Miss Matlock, this isn't a game. We could be tracking a desperate man." He rubbed his forehead. "I saw a young woman awhile ago, probably not much more than nineteen or twenty, who was beaten within an inch of her life by some man on a dark night. What if something like that was to happen to you? You don't know what kind of trouble we might find on the trail or in the next town we come to."

"I'm not going back until we find Bob, and if you leave me in Twin Springs, I shall simply follow you on my own." Panic welled inside of her. "I won't be left behind, Mr. Newman. I *can't* be left behind."

He made a sound, part groan, part growl. "You're a difficult woman, Miss Matlock."

"So my stepmother tells me."

One eyebrow rose a bit higher than the other as Jared looked at her, his thoughts inscrutable. Finally he said, "Mount up. We'll get rooms at the Colorado Hotel for the night."

Relief eased her panic. She'd won this particular battle. The bounty hunter might try to send her home again tomorrow or the next day or the day after that, but for now he was letting her stay.

Why Jared found it hard to say no to Silver Matlock, he couldn't fathom. It had to be more than her pretty face and expressive eyes. He'd never let a woman's looks alone sway him. In fact, no female in years had gotten the better of him the way Silver did. Not since Katrina.

As he lay on his bed in the hotel room, muffled sounds from the street below drifting through the closed window, he allowed himself to dwell on memories of his little sister. To remember the sparkle in her blue eyes and that particular smile she'd worn when she was determined to get her way. To remember the sound of her laughter that used to ring through Fair Acres at all hours of the day. To remember her winsome ways.

Katrina Newman had been the prettiest girl in the county, and while undoubtedly spoiled by her parents and her older brothers, she'd had the sweetest nature and the kindest of hearts. If the war hadn't taken away so many young men of Kentucky, she might have been married, and if she'd been married, she might have been far from the Newman home when a killer came calling.

Clenching his jaw, Jared drove away the painful memories. They served no good purpose. They wouldn't give him back the family he'd loved nor put his life on a different path than the one he walked.

There was only one thing he needed to think about now—the man with the crescent-shaped scar. He'd been in Central City just the previous week. He might not be far even now. Jared couldn't let him slip through his fingers yet again. Which meant he didn't have the time to look for a two-bit thief like Bob Cassidy.

Trouble was, Jared had given his word to Silver, and as much as he'd changed—for the worst, no doubt—over the years, as much as his heart had hardened toward people and life itself, at his core he remained the son of parents who'd taught him the importance of keeping his promises, the son of people who'd wanted him to be a man of integrity and honor.

Both of which were an inconvenience at a time like this.

Chapter 9

Jared was awake and dressed when the message arrived from Claudette, telling him he could see Felicity again. He wasted no time in going. He didn't even stop to inform Silver of his mission.

When he arrived at the Crystal Palace, he found Claudette waiting for him at the top of the stairs. “Felicity wants to speak with you alone. But if you do anything to upset her . . .” She shook her head, her warning clear.

“I won’t upset her. You have my word.”

The woman didn’t look convinced, but she motioned him toward the bedroom where he’d visited Felicity the previous day. He knocked on the door and waited for a response.

“Come in.”

Entering the room, he saw that Felicity was propped up by a number of fluffy pillows on the bed. A bright red scarf covered her shorn locks, but there was no hiding her swollen, bruised face.

“Good morning, miss.” He left the door ajar behind him.

“Morning.” She winced, as if it hurt to move her lips even a little.

Jared pulled a chair from against the wall and set it near the bed. Not too close. He didn’t want to make her feel threatened. “Thanks for letting me come back. I know it isn’t easy to talk about what happened. I can see you’re still scared. But there might be something you know that will help me find the man who hurt you. Some small detail you don’t even think is important. I want to find him. I want to make sure he isn’t able to do this to another woman ever again.”

Felicity swallowed and turned her head toward the window, where morning sunshine spilled through the curtains. "I was on my way home last week. It was late . . . and the night was dark."

It was difficult to wait for her to tell the story in her own way, at her own pace, but somehow Jared kept silent.

"He came up . . . behind me. Suddenly. I had . . . I had no warning. He put his hand over my mouth . . . and then . . . then he dragged me into an old shed. There was . . . there was a lantern . . . but it didn't shed much light. I fought him. I fought as hard as I could . . . but it was no use. Then he . . . he—" She broke off, unable to speak the unspeakable.

Jared understood without the words.

The room fell silent except for the ticking of a clock on a table against the opposite wall. It was a silence filled with pain. Jared wished he could touch her hand, offer her comfort, but such a gesture wouldn't be appreciated. Not in her fragile state. Not with the assault so fresh in her mind.

At long last Felicity drew a ragged breath and continued. "He talked. He talked all the time. And . . . and when he was . . . done, he beat me and . . . and cut off my hair. I asked him why . . . but he only laughed." She shuddered. "I thought . . . I thought he meant to kill me."

Sometimes this man killed his victims. Sometimes he let them live. Either way, he destroyed lives. The need for revenge coiled in Jared's gut, hot and furious.

Felicity met his gaze with her one good eye. "He thought I would die . . . before I was found. Didn't he? He thought I would die or he would have . . . made certain—" She stopped, and something about her expression altered.

Alert, Jared leaned forward on the chair. "What is it? What are you thinking?"

"I remembered something. He . . . he said he was going to be . . . the next king of the Comstock."

King of the Comstock? Comstock. The silver mines. Virginia City. Virginia City, Nevada.

At last. A real clue. At last he was back on the killer's trail. The man he'd sought for six years was headed to Nevada. And that was where Jared was headed too.

Silver Matlock, Bob Cassidy, and Matt Carlton be hanged.

Silver poured water from the pitcher into a porcelain bowl on the table beside the bureau. After washing the best she could, she dried off with a towel and donned her clothes. Then she frowned at her reflection in the mirror. There were gray smudges beneath her eyes, evidence of another sleepless night, and she looked unusually pale. She pinched her cheeks, trying to bring some color into them. It wouldn't do to have

Mr. Newman think she was ill. He was looking for any excuse to be rid of her.

A sharp rap on the door caused her to start.

"Are you up, Miss Matlock?" Jared asked from the hallway.

"Yes." She hurried across the room to open the door. "I'm up."

He looked at her, his expression dour. "Meet me out front in five minutes. We're leaving."

"Leaving? Did you learn—"

"Five minutes." He pivoted and walked toward the staircase.

Five minutes meant no breakfast. At the thought, her stomach growled. But she wasn't about to complain or keep him waiting. She grabbed her saddlebags and hurried after him. When she passed the hotel restaurant, she held her breath, pretending she hadn't already caught a whiff of fried bacon, cooked eggs, hot breads, and coffee. Once outside, she stopped, closed her eyes, and took a deep breath of crisp mountain air. If Jared Newman could go without a proper breakfast, so could she. He wouldn't have a single reason to regret taking her along. Not a single one.

Opening her eyes again, she saw their horses were tied to the rail right outside the hotel. Which meant the bounty hunter had gone to the livery stables before coming for her. Had he had time to eat too?

Her stomach growled a second time.

I won't complain. I won't say anything about being hungry.

Jared straightened from the other side of the packhorse, where she assumed he'd been checking their supplies. "Are you ready?" he asked.

"I'm ready."

"Then mount up. We're wasting daylight."

She bit back a retort. If she could look for Bob Cassidy without anyone's help, she would do it in a heartbeat, but she didn't even know where to begin. She was stuck with Mr. Newman. She would have to get used to his disagreeable nature.

Within minutes they were on their way, and as soon as they were beyond the last row of houses and businesses of Black Hawk, Jared kicked his gelding into an easy canter. Silver didn't have to ask Cinder to keep up. The buckskin did so on her own.

The sun had climbed a good distance before Jared finally slowed his horse to a walk.

Silver rode up beside him before doing the same. "Do you mind telling me where we're going? Do we have a destination?"

"Nevada."

"Why Nevada? Last night you said no one knew where Bob was going other than west."

He turned a hard gaze in her direction. "Nevada is west of here, and that's where we're headed."

Something about the set of his jaw told Silver she'd best not press him for more information.

"It's not too late to return to your parents' home in Twin Springs, Miss Matlock."

She shook her head. "I'm not going back."

"We're talking better than a thousand miles and more than a month on horseback. And that's assuming all goes well on the journey. We may not even find the man you seek when we get to Nevada. This could be a wild-goose chase we're on. He could be traveling by stage or train, something we can't afford to do. At least my funds are limited. What about yours?"

She thought of the locket beneath her blouse. They could sell it. What it brought, plus the emergency money her father had given her—when he'd thought she was bound for Denver—might be enough to secure train passage and cover the additional expenses they would surely incur. But what if they spent it all and still didn't find Bob? Or what if they found him but the money and jewels were gone?

"Well?" Jared prompted.

"No, I don't have the money for train fare, but if we have to go all the way to Nevada on horseback to find Bob, then so be it. I'm up to it if you are."

A faint, almost indiscernible guilt tugged at Jared's conscience. He ignored it. There'd been a day when lying to a woman as he'd just lied to Silver Matlock would have been unthinkable. Those days were long past. Lies came easily to a man in his profession. Subterfuge was a way of life.

It couldn't bother him that she believed it was Bob Cassidy and Matt Carlton he had in his sights. What troubled him was that he was letting her continue on with him. It made no sense. Of course, he'd met Mrs. Matlock—a most disagreeable woman with a sharp tongue, the kind who gave stepmothers a bad reputation—before leaving Twin Springs, so he couldn't blame Silver for not wanting to go home. But did she have to become his responsibility?

He'd lost his mind. That was the only explanation for his inability to send her back. They had just enough supplies to see them through a couple of weeks, maybe a bit more if they were careful. If the weather stayed good and none of the horses broke down and their luck held in every way, he figured they could reach Virginia City by early July. Alone, Jared could ride farther and faster. With a woman tagging along? It would take him days, maybe even weeks longer. Extra time when he might lose all traces of the killer he sought.

And yet he couldn't make Silver go back to Twin Springs. He'd let her get under his skin. That hadn't happened to him in years. Since leaving Fair Acres, he'd remained focused, determined, single-minded, his emotions always cool and controlled. Yet this young woman had managed to bypass his defenses with surprising ease.

He toyed with the idea of first riding into Denver to check with Rick Cooper about the reward for Peterson. But that would be a waste of time. Nothing involving government entities was ever straightened out quickly. He'd be lucky if the reward awaited him when he returned from Nevada weeks or months from now.

No, he wouldn't take the extra time to go into Denver. He wouldn't take the time to escort Silver home to Twin Springs. They would ride northeast until they were out of the mountains. From there they would head north into Wyoming, skirting the highest of the Rocky Mountains, then finally head west again.

And Silver Matlock had better keep up.

Chapter 10

A relentless afternoon sun beat down on the travelers, the temperature much warmer than normal for May. Trickles of sweat ran along Silver's back and the sides of her face. Her empty stomach seemed to have flattened itself against her spine. Would Jared ever stop to eat something? It seemed a lifetime since she'd had some food.

Dust rose behind the packhorse's hooves to stick to her damp skin. Her eyes stung and her nostrils felt clogged with dirt despite the bandanna she wore over her nose and mouth. Even swallowing was difficult; her throat was parched and in need of a long drink of water. But she wouldn't complain. Not for anything in the world. She'd told the bounty hunter she could handle it if he could, and so she would.

But at last, with deep shadows stretching toward the east, Jared slowed his mount from a trot to a walk and glanced over his shoulder. "We'll stop at the stream ahead to water the horses. But I'd like to go another hour before we make camp for the night."

Relief and disappointment mingled in her chest as she acknowledged his words with a nod. She welcomed the chance to wash the dust from her face and from her throat and wished they could make camp in this spot as well.

The trail sloped down a rocky hillside toward the creek. There was no need to guide the horses toward it; they were as thirsty as their riders. Silver gave Cinder her head as she leaned over and reached for the canteen.

The ground below began to undulate. Wavy lines of white and black danced before her eyes.

She straightened in the saddle, willing the weird sensation to go away, but it was too late. A moment later she pitched into a dark vortex that sucked her down . . . down . . . down . . .

She was in Twin Springs, in the church, wearing her wedding gown. The sanctuary was filled with flowers, the pews decorated with white satin bows. But there were no guests to be seen, no pastor in his black robe standing near the altar. A sickening sensation swirled inside her, making her dizzy and frightened. The bows disappeared. The flowers were no longer there. It wasn't her church after all. It felt more like a barn or a cavern. Dark and dangerous—

"Miss Matlock?"

The darkness suffocated her . . .

"Miss Matlock, look at me."

It took great effort to obey the voice.

"That's it. Look at me. Keep your eyes open. That's better."

Slowly she became aware of her surroundings and realized her right cheek rested against Jared's chest. She felt the rhythm of his heart through his shirt, a comforting sound. Beyond him, a leafy aspen whispered in the breeze.

"What happened?" she asked.

"You fell off your horse. I think you fainted."

She swallowed. "Don't be absurd. I've never fainted in my life."

"There's a first time for everything." He chuckled.

A strange feeling curled in her stomach. He appeared almost . . . handsome. Her eyes focused on his mustache, on his mouth, on the smile that curved his lips, and she couldn't seem to look away.

"Here. You'd better take a sip of water." He braced her head as he held the canteen to her lips. "Not too much. Take small sips."

She closed her eyes, enjoying the feel of the water on her tongue and in her throat.

"Want to try sitting up a little more?"

She looked at him again and was surprised by what she found. His eyes weren't hard and remote as she'd often thought them. She saw warmth, perhaps even a hint of kindness. And his smile was pleasant, inviting.

"Okay, Miss Matlock." His left arm tightened around her back, his hand gripping her shoulder as he drew her upright. "That's better."

She liked the sound of his soft southern drawl. And the way he held her, almost tenderly—

"Do you think you're injured?" he asked. "You took quite a tumble."

Embarrassment rushed through her. "I . . . I'm quite all right, Mr. Newman. I was hot and hungry and . . ." She let her words drift into silence.

His smile faded. He released his hold and stood. "I pushed you too hard. I knew better." He turned, perusing their surroundings. Finally he pointed toward a copse of Gambel oak and mountain mahogany. "We'll make camp over there. I'll take care of the horses and get a fire going, and you can put on a pot of coffee."

Silver waited until he'd walked away before she got to her feet. The dizziness had passed, but she discovered a few bruised places—her left shoulder and hip especially—that she suspected would become more painful before tomorrow morning.

Why, oh why, had she done something so stupid? Fainting! Falling off her horse! That was the sort of thing her stepsister would do, but Silver wasn't given to—what did they call it?—the vapors. Contrary to the common opinion of the day, she didn't believe women were fundamentally weak or more susceptible to medical complaints than men. True, there were some things she wasn't able to do because of her size and weight. But match her with a man of equal height and build, and she could hold her own.

Stupid, stupid, stupid.

She brushed the dirt from her riding skirt and followed Jared to their campsite. It took her longer than she would have liked to locate the coffeepot, coffee beans, and brass grinder among the other supplies. After she did, she went to the nearby stream and filled the blue-speckled pot with water. A fire was blazing by the time she returned. Jared now tended to the horses.

How many beans should she grind for a single

pot? She'd watched her parents make coffee in the morning for most of her life, but she hadn't paid attention to the process. She couldn't ask Jared. Not after her fall from the saddle. He already thought her a nuisance. No, she would have to make her best guess and hope she was right.

Silver knew slightly more about cooking than she did about preparing coffee. She returned to the supplies, retrieving a can of kidney beans and two pork steaks her father had packed in salt. The steaks went into the frying pan. She was smart enough to know there wouldn't be many meals on the trail where they'd eat as well as this. Hardtack and jerky would be their fare more often than not. She supposed Jared was used to such limited choices.

She supposed he was used to lots of things she couldn't imagine. A shiver ran through her at the thought. It should have served as a warning to keep her distance, but instead it made her want to know him better. It made her want—

"Is that coffee about ready?"

She felt a blush warm her cheeks and was thankful for the failing light of day. "Yes, I think it is." She set down the fork she'd used to turn the steaks in the frying pan and picked up a tin cup, filling it with the hot, black brew.

Jared accepted it from her outstretched hand before settling onto a fallen log. He blew across the steaming coffee. “Smells good.” He motioned with his head toward the frying pan.

“The steaks should be ready soon. The beans are hot by now.”

He nodded. “We’ll get an early start in the morning, soon as the sun’s up.”

“I’ll be ready.”

“How are you feeling?”

She turned the pork steaks again. “More foolish than hurt.”

After blowing across the surface of his cup one more time, Jared took a long sip. Immediately his eyes widened and he began to cough. “What’s in this?” he asked when he caught his breath.

“Coffee.”

“Coffee? This would eat a hole clean through the leather of my saddle. How much did you put in there anyway?”

How Silver longed to give him a piece of her mind. If he didn’t like her coffee, he could make his own. She hadn’t volunteered to be his cook. She was paying *him*. He should cook for her.

She swallowed an angry retort, resolved not to make another mistake today. She wouldn’t let her temper make her more foolish in his eyes. Not even if he insulted her ten ways to Sunday.

They ate their meal in silence, Jared on one side of the campfire and Silver on the other. The only sounds were the clink of utensils against tin plates, the crackle of the fire, and an occasional snort or stomp from one of the horses.

Jared figured he should apologize. He knew he'd wounded her pride and made her angry. Although she tried to hide her feelings, they were written on her face. He wondered if she knew what a pretty face it was. Something in her manner told him she didn't.

What surprised him was that for all the trouble she'd caused him, he'd started to like Silver Matlock. She had gumption. Even when she was afraid or unsure, she tried her best. She gave her all. He admired that in any person. In addition, Silver hadn't once tried to use feminine charms to get her way. Maybe she didn't know she had any. He wasn't going to be the one to point them out to her.

He cleared his throat. "Sorry I insulted your coffee."

It was a while before she lifted her eyes to meet his. "You were right. It is terrible." She drew in a breath and let it out on a sigh. "I should have asked for help since I didn't know what I was doing. I'm not very good at that."

"At what? Asking for help?"

She nodded.

They resumed eating. When they were finished, the two of them, by unspoken accord, carried their dishes and cookware to the stream and washed them. Rising from the creek's edge, Silver emitted a groan.

"Some liniment might help with those sore muscles," Jared offered.

"I'll be all right."

"Not very good at asking for help. Isn't that what you said?"

After a brief hesitation, she laughed, a pleasant sound. "That's what I said."

"We all have them. Failings, I mean."

"So we do." She started walking toward the fire. "But I seem to have more than my share. God must grow quite weary trying to fix me."

He was tempted to follow her, to keep the conversation going. Which surprised him a second time. Years on the trail had made him comfortable with his own thoughts for company. He'd become used to the silence on a starlit night, just him and his horses. But before he could join her near the campfire, it occurred to him that she would probably like some privacy as she prepared to bed down for the night. Better to let her be. Better for them both.

"Miss Matlock, I'm going to check on the horses, then take a short walk. I'll be back in about ten minutes or so."

"Thank you, Mr. Newman."

By the time he returned to the campsite, Silver lay beneath the blankets of her bedroll, her arms folded beneath her head as she stared at the night sky. The fire had died down, hot coals casting a reddish glow for a few feet in all directions.

Jared unbuckled his gun belt and placed a weapon within easy reach of his bedroll. Then he dropped to the ground and pulled the blanket up to his shoulders. Like Silver, he stared at the sky. New leaves rustled in the nearby trees, and in the distance a coyote's mournful cry drifted to them on the night breeze. One of the horses nickered, another snorted. Familiar sights and sounds. No signs of danger.

"I didn't love Bob," Silver said softly, regret in her words. "That's another of my many faults. Rushing headlong into disasters of my own making. But I thought what I felt for him was enough for us to have a good marriage. I truly believed that. And I made myself believe that he loved me. At the least, I believed he was serious when he asked me to marry him. I never thought he would break his word."

An odd feeling stirred in Jared's chest, an emotion he couldn't describe. But he could recognize the sense of guilt that nagged at him. Guilt because he no longer sought the groom who'd abandoned her in the church. He was after another man, a man with a distinctive scar. If they should happen upon Silver's former fiancé in the process, then all the better, but Bob was no longer Jared's priority.

Her last words were barely audible. "I was such a fool to think he could love me."

Jared wasn't sure, but he thought what he heard next might be a muffled sob, the sound almost hidden by the coyote's late-night wail.

Chapter 11

Silver awakened to the sound of bacon sizzling in the skillet. She sat up, pushing her tangled hair from her face.

"Morning," Jared said.

The sky was pewter in color, the air crisp and cold. It seemed a much better idea to stay snuggled beneath her blankets until the sun was full up and had a chance to warm the earth.

"Better get moving, Miss Matlock. We'll want to be on our way as soon as we eat. The weather's good, and we should be able to cover a lot of ground before nightfall."

Silver rose from her bedroll and stumbled off in the general direction of the stream. Perhaps she would feel human again once she'd splashed water on her face. Then again, she doubted it. Her body ached from head to toe—from yesterday's long hours in the saddle or from her tumble from the saddle or from last night's bed on the hard, uneven ground. More likely from all three.

She knelt beside the brook. Oh, how she wished

she could take a real bath. Her stepmother's pride and joy in the Matlock home was a separate bathing room, and Silver had made good use of it in recent years. She loved soaking in hot water, steam swirling around her face, oftentimes reading a book until the water grew too cool to remain in the tub. Now she would gladly settle for a pan of warm water and a door to close behind her. She would get neither.

"Food's about ready, Miss Matlock."

Silver unbuttoned the neck of her blouse and rolled up her sleeves. Scooping icy water into her hands, she washed her neck, arms, and face. Next she loosened what hair remained in a braid, brushed it, and braided it once again.

"Your breakfast's getting cold."

Once again, she swallowed the retort that came so quickly to mind. "I'll only be a few minutes more." She moved toward some trees and high brush, seeking more privacy.

"Be careful you don't startle any rattlers."

Rattlesnakes? Why did he have to put that thought into her head? She hated snakes, poisonous and otherwise. A shudder passed through her as she fastened her gaze on the ground, moving with much more care than she had before.

When she returned to the campsite a short while later, she found her breakfast waiting on a plate near the fire. The frying pan had been washed, and Jared was putting it back in its place on the packhorse. Sensing his impatience, she sat down and made short shrift of the bacon and biscuits, washing the food down with coffee that had grown cool in the tin cup—but which still tasted better than the brew she'd made the previous night.

Jared returned to the campfire. "Ready?"

She nodded as she swallowed the last bite on her plate.

He smothered the fire with sand and dirt, then poured the last of the coffee over the coals before stirring them with a stick, making sure the fire was completely extinguished. "Time we were out of here. I'd like to reach Laramie by Tuesday. Wednesday at the latest. That means we'll have to keep pushing ourselves and the horses hard."

Silver stood. "I'll saddle Cinder as soon as I rinse these dishes." She hurried to the stream.

Jared maintained a steady pace throughout the day, resting only when necessary for the horses. If he'd had the money to buy fresh mounts when needed, he wouldn't have rested even then. He'd learned long ago that he could go without much sleep for several days if the need arose, but the horses had to eat and rest if he didn't want them to break down.

He didn't ask Silver how she fared. He didn't encourage conversation of any kind. He told her when it was time to stop and when it was time to continue. He expected to hear her voice a complaint, but she never did. Not one word. Not one plea to slow down or request to rest a little longer or wish for better food. And no more fainting spells either. His admiration for her grit continued to grow.

When they finally stopped for the night, Silver took care of her mare while Jared saw to the two other horses. Once the animals were hobbled and able to graze, Jared started a fire and made a pot of coffee. He couldn't help noticing how closely Silver watched as he spooned the ground coffee beans into the pot, and he was certain the next time she made the brew, it would be fit to drink.

Working together, they prepared a simple meal for dinner and settled on their respective bedrolls to eat it. Neither said anything until their tin plates were clean. It was Silver who broke the silence.

"Tell me about yourself, Mr. Newman."

"Not much to tell." He set his plate aside.

"I doubt that's true."

He offered a half smile. "Maybe I should've said not much of interest to tell."

"I don't believe that either. Tell me about your home. Where are you from?"

It had been a long time since anyone had asked him that question. Years, in fact. Which suited him fine. The past wasn't something he cared to share with others.

"We're going to be traveling together for many days, Mr. Newman. Perhaps even weeks. It would be nice to know each other a little better. Don't you think so?"

He had good reasons not to answer her, but something about the way she looked at him compelled him to speak. "I'm from Kentucky."

A smile flickered across her face. "I thought I heard that in your voice."

"My family had a horse farm. Fair Acres. One of the largest before the war."

His had been a perfect boyhood. Green pastures and whitewashed fences. Mares and foals cantering through belly-high grass. Sunny afternoons spent swinging on ropes from tree limbs with his brothers and friends and splashing naked into the pond. The shadowy barns filled with hay and straw, the pungent odors of dung and sweat in the air. Fresh lemonade served in the shade of the wide veranda, his mother smelling of honeysuckle toilet water.

"My father and my grandfather before him raised Thoroughbreds."

"To race?"

Jared nodded. "Before the war."

"And after?"

"There weren't many horses left at Fair Acres after the war. The Confederacy took most of them. The breeding mares and stallions included."

"How awful. Is that why you left Kentucky?"

He thought of his mother, father, and sister as he'd last seen them, lying in their coffins. "No, that isn't why I left." He heard the hard edge in his reply and hoped she'd heard it too. Maybe then she wouldn't continue.

He wasn't that lucky.

"Don't you miss your family?"

"I have no family left to miss." He reached for his dinner plate and stood.

"No one?" She rose as well. "I'm sorry, Mr. Newman. I can only imagine how hard that must be, to lose the people you love."

With a nod, he reached out and took the plate from her hands. "I'll take care of the dishes. You get ready to turn in. We'll be on our way at sunrise."

He turned and walked to the stream.

That night Silver dreamed about horses. Hundreds of Thoroughbreds galloping across rolling fields of green. Black horses, sorrel horses, buckskins and palominos and roans. Big stallions and young foals and pregnant mares.

She ran with them. Right in the midst of the herd. Feet soaring over the ground. Her hair whipped out behind her like a horse's tail in the wind. She felt wild and free. Laughter blossomed in her heart, although she made no sound.

Everything was beautiful in the dream, from the bright yellow sun in a powder-blue sky to the brook running through the pastures. Joy. She felt a joy she'd never felt before. Oh, the freedom!

But then the horses turned in a tight circle and came to a halt. Their heads came up, and they all looked in the same direction at once.

That's when she saw him, the man on horseback. He wore a hat that shaded his face from view as his horse loped toward her. She knew him and yet she didn't know him. He was a stranger to her and yet he seemed somehow familiar. Perhaps it was the way he sat on his horse. Perhaps it was the breadth of his shoulders. In a moment she would know who it was. In a short while she would see his face.

Her heart beat faster and faster. Faster even than when she'd run with the herd.

Whoever he was, he was coming for her.

Yes! I'm ready! Hurry!

Chapter 12

Jared and Silver were on the trail before the sun rose in the east. It had been only two days since they'd left Central City, but already they'd settled on a morning routine that was both fast and efficient. They rode in a silence that was becoming familiar to Silver. Many times she would think of something she wanted to say to Jared or wished to ask him, but more often than not she swallowed the words and retreated into her own thoughts.

And those thoughts were usually about the man riding ahead of her. Jared had called her difficult when she refused to return to Twin Springs, but if she was difficult, so was he. Still, he could have refused her request to go with him. Or, worse yet, he could have left her in Central City or abandoned her on the trail during the night. Some men would have done that. But not Jared Newman. His profession might not be highly esteemed and he might hate having her tag along, but he remained a man of his word.

It had been hard for him to talk about Fair Acres, about the horses being taken during the war, about his family being dead. Whether because he was a private man or because he'd been on his own too long, he didn't like to talk about himself. She'd seen it in the set of his jaw and the look in his eyes, and she'd been moved with compassion for him.

What had happened to his family? Had they died in the war or after? Why had he left Kentucky? What made a man with his background become a bounty hunter? Those questions and more swirled in her mind as they rode north, the Rocky Mountains on their left, the plains of eastern Colorado to their right.

As morning passed, her thoughts drifted on, this time to her previous night's dream. It had been fresh in her mind when she'd awakened, so fresh she remembered it now as if she'd just dreamed it. How wonderful it had been, running with the horses. Almost as if she'd taken flight. No fear. Only joy and exhilaration and freedom. And that man on the horse. Her heart quickened at the memory, but she tried to squelch the response.

Hadn't she learned anything from her experience with Bob? Was she so starved for affection that she would dream up a mystery man to fill the void? Of course not. She didn't need or want a man in her life. She'd learned her lesson with Bob. She was through with men. She would never marry.

And besides, dreams were meaningless.

Jared turned in his saddle to look back at her. "There's a creek up ahead. We'll rest the horses and eat."

Her breath caught in her throat. She hadn't remembered it until now, but the man in her dream had been riding a black-and-white pinto. Just like Jared's. The man had sat on his horse in the same way. Those shoulders. The way he wore his hat.

Merciful heavens! Jared Newman was the man in her dream.

He slowed his horse, allowing her to ride up

beside him. “Is something wrong, Miss Matlock?”

“No.” She gave her head a small shake. “But I think a rest is a good idea.”

Jared wondered what was going on in Silver’s head. Since stopping to rest the horses and eat, she had avoided looking him in the eyes, almost as if she were afraid of him. But why? He hadn’t spoken a harsh word to her all morning, and he hadn’t threatened to send her back to Twin Springs in at least two days. But something was bothering her. She was as skittish as a green-broke colt.

While the horses grazed, Jared and Silver sat on opposite ends of a log near the stream and ate a lunch of hardtack and beef jerky. Silver sat with her back angled toward Jared. It surprised him to discover how bothered he was by her cool silence.

Deciding to put an end to it, he cleared his throat. “We ought to reach Laramie by day after tomorrow.”

“That’s good.”

“Maybe we’ll be lucky and someone will have seen Mr. Cassidy and Mr. Carlton when they passed through there.”

“*If* they passed through there. And we don’t know for certain they’re traveling together. Isn’t that what you told me?”

“If Bob Cassidy is headed for Nevada—and I

have reason to believe that's the destination—he'll have passed through Laramie." He was lying to her again. But what else could he do?

She twisted on the log, meeting his gaze at last. "Even if they're together, they might have taken a southern route."

"It's possible, but not likely."

"We may have lost any trace of Bob and his friend already."

"True enough."

Her cheeks paled. "Do you really believe so?"

He could have told her that he'd been searching for one fugitive from justice for six years, that he'd lost and found that particular man's trail numerous times over the course of those years. At least she knew what Bob Cassidy looked like. Jared had only the vaguest of physical descriptions of the man he sought. Except for the scar . . . and what he did to his victims.

"Is it hopeless, then?" Silver asked softly.

Maybe he'd be rid of her if he answered in the affirmative. Maybe she would give up and go home to Twin Springs. But oddly enough, he didn't seem to want that. "No, Miss Matlock. I don't believe it's hopeless." The words were true, as far as they went. Jared would ask about the two men traveling together, even though finding them was no longer his first priority.

Silver sighed as she raised her eyes toward the sky. "How I wish I'd never met Bob Cassidy."

Jared found himself wishing the same thing. "Can't any of us undo our past." He remembered all too well the thoughts that had haunted him after he'd discovered his murdered parents and dying sister. Perhaps if he'd been at home, he could have stopped the killer. Or perhaps he would have been the fourth victim. More than once he'd wished he had been. He'd even begged God to strike him dead rather than let him live with the pain, rage, and loneliness.

The Almighty hadn't answered that prayer, and as far as he could recall, that had been the last time he'd asked God for anything.

He stood. "We'd best be on our way again, Miss Matlock. The sooner we reach Laramie, the sooner we might have answers."

Chapter 13

Laramie had appeared on the Wyoming prairie in the 1860s, a tent city near the Overland Stage route. By the time the first Union Pacific train arrived there in 1868—close to a year before the transcontinental railroad was completed at Promontory, Utah—more permanent buildings had begun to appear. But even five years later, with a school and churches, homes and stores, Laramie retained its reputation for lawlessness.

It was late in the afternoon when Silver and

Jared guided their horses across the railroad tracks beneath the shadow of the towering windmill and water tank. Silver looked at every building, wondering if Bob might be inside one of them. Could she be lucky enough to find him this soon? Even if she found him, would she recover what he'd taken from her father? And would recovering what Bob stole be enough to redeem herself in her parents' eyes? If people in Twin Springs learned she hadn't been with her sister in Denver but instead had been alone on the trail with a bounty hunter—

Well, that didn't bear thinking about. And besides, she didn't care what they thought. Nothing inappropriate had happened. Nothing inappropriate *would* happen. How could it? Jared Newman hardly seemed to know she was alive, let alone that she was a woman. Which was fine with her.

As they rode past a hotel, her thoughts changed abruptly. What she wouldn't give for a hot bath and a night between real sheets on a soft mattress. It felt like a year rather than days since they'd stayed at the Colorado Hotel in Central City.

Jared stopped his pinto in front of Mabel's Restaurant in the center of town. "You go in and order us some dinner. I'll ride over to the train station and see what I can find out."

"I'll come with you."

"No. I prefer to do this alone."

Too tired to argue with him, she stepped down from the saddle. "What do you want to eat?"

"Doesn't matter. Whatever you decide you want, I'll have the same."

She wrapped the mare's reins around the hitching rail, then reached for the packhorse's lead rope and did the same. Jared nudged his gelding toward the depot and rode away without another word.

Silver was on the boardwalk, about to enter the restaurant, when she heard a woman's voice exclaim, "Jared Newman! As I live and breathe!"

She turned in time to see Jared stop his pinto, then quickly dismount. A moment later he embraced the petite woman. Silver couldn't see her face, but she wore a pale brown dress, and her strawberry blonde hair peeked from beneath a straw hat. Jared's expression as he released his hold said that he was more than a little glad to see her.

Something twisted in Silver's belly.

The woman took hold of Jared's hand and led him toward the nearby saloon, pausing only long enough to let him tie up his horse.

Silver's mouth dropped open. Hadn't he been in a hurry to go to the train depot to ask questions? And why so quick to go with that woman into the saloon? Did a pretty face make him forget his hunger and his mission? Obviously so. Well, Silver hadn't forgotten what needed done.

It didn't take a genius to inquire if someone had seen Bob. She could do it herself.

She set off in the direction of the train station.

It had been better than four years since Jared had seen Whitney Hanover and her husband, Tom. They'd lived in Kansas at the time. The Hanovers were two of the few people Jared could call real friends and not just acquaintances.

"What are you doing in Laramie?" he asked Whitney as she drew him through the swinging doors of the saloon.

"We live here now." She motioned with her hand. "We own the Red Dog Saloon."

Jared swept the room with his gaze. "Where's Tom?"

"Over at the bank. He'll be back soon. Please, sit down and wait for him. He wouldn't forgive me if I let you get away before he could see you."

Jared obliged, taking a chair beside a green felt–covered card table. He looked around the room a second time. Since it was empty of customers, it appeared the Red Dog was not a popular establishment. "How long have you been here?"

"About three years now. Nothing was the same in Topeka, even after you helped clear Tom's name. So we decided to pack up and start over again farther west. Tom worked for the railroad for a while. That's how we came to be in Laramie.

When we had the chance to buy this saloon, we decided to stay for good."

"A lot different from owning a millinery shop, isn't it?"

She laughed. "Very. But more profitable. A woman can always find a reason to put off buying a new hat, but men seem to like their liquor no matter what."

Jared glanced toward the bar. How could it be profitable without customers?

Whitney must have read his mind. "We're closed today because of a funeral in town. We'll open up at seven tonight."

He looked at her again. She wore a simple and prim brown dress, and her face still had the innocent, well-scrubbed appearance that he remembered. "I can't quite picture you working in a saloon, Whitney."

"I don't work in it. I keep the accounts upstairs while Tom tends to business in the saloon. We're happy here. It suits us."

"I'm glad to find you so content. It's obvious that leaving Kansas was a good decision. Your smile tells me that." He grinned. "And Tom's a wise man. If you were my wife, I'd keep you out of sight too. Much too pretty for your own good."

She blushed a pretty pink. "The saloon isn't why I'm so happy. It's motherhood that's done that. Tom and I have a son. Thomas Jr. We call him TJ. He's two and keeps me running all the time."

A son. Jared grinned at the news.

Four years ago Tom Hanover's life had been a total shambles. Accused of murder, he'd depended on Jared discovering and bringing in the real killer and clearing his name. Whitney had sold her hat shop and their home to pay for her husband's legal defense and Jared's services. But the tide of public opinion had turned against Tom the same way some so-called friends had turned away. Many of those same people, after Tom was cleared of the crime, were too embarrassed by their behavior to act like friends again.

But from Whitney's look, they'd put that dark time behind them. They'd started over, with new hopes and new dreams and even a new family.

He was surprised to realize he envied the Hanovers.

The railroad station clerk behind the counter peered at Silver over the rim of his glasses. "Who'd you say you was lookin' for?"

She swallowed a sigh. "Their names are Mr. Cassidy and Mr. Carlton. But it's possible they aren't traveling together. If they are, they may have purchased their tickets here in Laramie to someplace farther west. We think it could be to Nevada."

"Miss, lots of people come through Laramie,

and I sure as shootin' don't meet 'em all or get their names." His eyes narrowed. "What're you lookin' for them for, anyhow?"

"It's a . . . a family matter." Her cheeks grew warm. "But it's urgent that I find Mr. Cassidy." She leaned forward, gripping the edge of the counter. "Please try to remember, sir. They would have come through Laramie within the last two weeks. Mr. Cassidy is a tall man, a little over six feet, and he's clean shaven. He has pale yellow hair and blue eyes." She touched her right eyebrow. "And he has a small white scar right here."

The clerk's expression altered. "Come to think of it, I guess I have seen the man you're lookin' for. But not here at the station. It was in town. He was at the Red Dog Saloon. Good-lookin' fellow with yella hair, just like you said. Not more'n five or six days ago. He was gamblin' heavy that night. I remember 'cause folks were still talkin' about it the next day."

Gambling? With her father's money. Had he lost?

As if hearing the question, the clerk added, "Ain't often the house loses, but they did that night."

"The house lost?"

"Your friend came out the winner at the table. Seems like there was another man with him."

She felt some of the tension leave her shoulders. "Do you know where they're staying?"

"Sorry. Far as I know, they left town. I'm pretty sure I'd've heard if the fella you're lookin' for was still around. Unless he decided to give up card playin'—and that's not very likely when a man's on a winnin' streak."

Silver took a step back from the counter. "Thank you for your help, sir. It's appreciated."

"It's possible they bought passage when I wasn't here. I'm not the only clerk."

"Thank you," she repeated before turning away.

Her heart was pumping fast by the time she returned to the center of town, intent on informing Jared of what she'd learned. It wasn't until she was almost to the saloon where she'd last seen him that she realized it was the same saloon where the railroad clerk said Bob had been gambling.

She ignored the Closed sign hanging on the hinged door, pushed the door open, and stepped inside. She stopped on the threshold. Save for Jared and the woman he'd embraced outside on the boardwalk, the large room was empty—no surprise since the saloon was closed for business. Jared and the pretty blonde were seated at a table not far from where Silver stood, enjoying what appeared to be an intimate conversation, just the two of them in the shadowy light of the saloon.

As if Jared had nothing better to do. As if he

hadn't been pushing hard to get to Laramie in as few days as possible only to forget why he'd come there. As if he hadn't agreed to find Bob Cassidy for the reward. As if Silver no longer existed.

"Mr. Newman."

Startled, Jared glanced up, then got to his feet. "Miss Matlock? What is it?"

"Bob was here in Laramie."

"Did someone at the restaurant tell you?"

"No, not at the restaurant. I learned it from the railroad clerk."

"I thought you were ordering our dinner."

If I had been, it would have gone cold before you remembered it. She lifted her chin. "I saw that you were busy here"—*with this woman*—"so I took it upon myself to begin the investigation without you."

Jared frowned as he moved toward her.

"Bob was in Laramie, in this saloon, just a few nights ago. Gambling." She took a breath. "With my father's money."

He glanced over his shoulder. "You said Tom will return soon?"

"Yes," the woman answered. "I'm not sure why it's taking him so long." She rose, walked to where Jared and Silver stood, and offered her hand to Silver. "Jared has forgotten his manners, so I'll introduce myself. I'm Whitney Hanover."

The woman, perhaps five years Silver's senior,

was even more attractive up close. Her complexion was flawless, her eyes a beautiful green, her figure perfection even in that plain brown dress. Men were surely drawn to her like bees to a flower. Silver felt the grime of the trail on her skin and wished she'd had a bath before telling Jared what she'd learned at the station.

"How do you do?" Reluctantly, she took hold of the proffered hand. "I'm Silver Matlock."

"Let's sit down, shall we? My husband should return any moment now."

Her husband. How strange that those words caused Silver's annoyance to vanish in an instant.

Tom Hanover's delight in seeing Jared was as genuine and heartfelt as his wife's had been. But Jared didn't allow them to spend much time in small talk.

"Tom, we're looking for a man. Someone"—he searched for the right word—"close to Miss Matlock." He glanced at Silver. "Tell him what Cassidy looks like."

She did so.

"Yes," Tom answered with a nod, "he was here. He played cards at our tables for several evenings in a row. The last time was three nights ago."

Three nights. They were closer than Jared had dared hope they might be. "Anyone else with him?"

"Yes. Although they might not have come in together. But they seemed well acquainted. Had their heads together a time or two. Other one was shorter, had hair a bit darker. He didn't seem any too happy, even with his friend winning big. Both of them were new to Laramie—or at least they were new to the Red Dog."

"Either of them still in town that you know of?"

Tom shook his head. "They took the westbound train out of Laramie on Saturday morning. I know because I was at the station, picking up a shipment that came in on the same train. I saw them board with about a dozen other folks. I'll admit, I wasn't sorry to see that Mr. Cassidy leave town. His winnings made a sizable cut into our profits."

It wasn't Bob Cassidy who had brought Jared to Laramie, but perhaps he'd be able to find the wayward fiancé for Silver while continuing his search for his true prey. Obviously Cassidy wasn't worried about anyone looking for him, or he wouldn't have made his presence in town so obvious. That kind of behavior would work in Jared's favor.

Whitney touched his arm with her fingertips, drawing his attention. "You and Miss Matlock must eat here and stay the night with us. We have rooms upstairs for you both."

"Yes," Tom chimed in. "You must stay. It's the least we can do for you after what you did for us."

Silver looked at Jared, curiosity in her gaze, obviously wondering what Jared had done for the Hanovers.

He ignored the look and nodded his assent to Tom. He wasn't about to look a gift horse in the mouth.

Chapter 14

Jared stepped onto the balcony overlooking the main thoroughfare. Voices and music from the Red Dog drifted upward to meet him. More of the same came from similar establishments farther down the street.

On nights like this, when sleep wouldn't come, when old memories rose up to torture him, he wished he could drown his thoughts in a bottle of whiskey. But he'd learned the hard way that he couldn't escape the past in a bottle. He could drink himself into oblivion, but nothing would have changed when he regained consciousness. Once he'd realized that truth, he'd become a teetotaler, focused not on forgetting but on finding. Finding the man who had taken his family from him. Finding him and getting revenge.

"Jared? You out there?"

He turned as Tom stepped through the doorway.

"I knocked on your door, but you didn't answer."

"Sorry. Didn't hear you."

Tom joined him at the railing, his gaze moving up and down the street. "Laramie's been good to us."

Jared nodded.

"Gotta say, I was hoping that by now you'd've found a girl and settled down."

"Not everyone's as lucky as you, Tom. Women like Whitney are few and far between."

"What about Miss Matlock?" Tom turned and leaned his backside against the balcony railing, crossing his arms over his chest. "Is there anything happening between you two?"

Jared chuckled as he shook his head. "No."

"Then why let her accompany you? Not exactly your style. I remember you saying you work best alone."

"Yeah, that's what I said." He turned his eyes toward the train station.

"Are you still looking for him?" There was no need for either of them to clarify whom Tom meant.

"Yeah, I'm still looking. He's the main reason I'm here."

"I take it Miss Matlock doesn't know that. She seems to think it's Mr. Cassidy who brought you to Laramie."

Jared shrugged. "I'm hoping to kill two birds with one stone. For now, at least, both men seem to be headed in the same direction."

"You think the man who murdered your family was in Laramie too?"

"Not sure. But the last I heard, Virginia City, Nevada, was his destination. I hoped someone might've seen him getting on the train here in Laramie and remembered that scar." He touched the hollow of his throat. "He almost killed another girl in Central City. There's no doubt it was him. I was only about a week behind him."

"The girl. She lived?"

"She lived."

"She was lucky."

Lucky didn't feel like the right word. It hadn't felt like the right word for years. There'd been people back in Kentucky—well-meaning neighbors and friends—who'd said that about him: *"Lucky you weren't at home, boy. You'd be dead too."*

"Wish I could be of some help," Tom said, intruding on Jared's thoughts. "But strangers come through Laramie every day. Just like that Cassidy fellow. Only reason I remembered him was because he won big at cards, and him you could describe. Hard to identify a man without more to go on than average height, dark blond hair, and a scar that could be hidden under any shirt."

"I know." Jared took a deep breath and let it out. "But eventually he'll make a mistake and I'll find him. Maybe it'll be someday soon."

"I hope so, for your sake." Tom patted his shoulder. "You deserve a better life than the one you have."

Silver answered the soft knock on the bedroom door. Whitney stood on the other side of the doorway.

"Sorry to disturb you, Miss Matlock. I wondered if there's anything you need to make you more comfortable?"

"Thank you, no. I have everything I need." She touched her still-damp hair. "And the bath was heavenly."

A breeze rustled the curtains over the open window and brought with it the muffled voices of two men on the balcony. Tom and Jared. Over supper in the Hanover suite earlier in the evening, Silver had learned a little about Jared and the young couple's friendship. Hearing the story of how Tom had been wrongfully accused of murder and how Jared had tracked down the real killer had made her see him in a new light. His work wasn't just about the bounty he earned when he brought in a criminal. According to the Hanovers, Jared was motivated by a need for justice above all else. It pleased her to know this about him. Perhaps pleased her more than it should.

Whitney said, "Jared says you'll leave at first light."

"Yes."

"Then I shouldn't keep you. You need to get a good night's rest."

"Mrs. Hanover—"

"Please. Call me Whitney."

Silver smiled, thinking it strange how much she'd disliked the woman when she first saw her and how much she liked her now. "Whitney. In case I haven't said it already, thanks so much for your hospitality. This"—she motioned toward the bed—"is a nice reprieve from sleeping on the ground."

"I would feel the same way. All those hours in the saddle, sleeping under the stars, risking life, limb, and the disapproval of others." Whitney started to turn away, then stopped and looked at Silver again. "You must love him a great deal."

"No, not at all. If I ever felt love for Bob Cassidy, he crushed that feeling on what should have been our wedding day. I feel nothing for him now but contempt."

Whitney's smile was gentle. "I didn't mean Mr. Cassidy. I meant Jared."

"Jared?" Silver felt her eyes go wide.

"I saw it on your face at supper. It was there whenever you looked at him."

"Whitney, believe me. You're wrong. I barely know Mr. Newman. I hired him to find Bob. That's all that's between us."

"Time isn't always what makes two people draw close to each other. Sometimes the heart understands far more than the mind, and much sooner too."

Silver wanted to protest again, but she seemed incapable of it.

Whitney offered another knowing smile. "Good night, Silver. Rest well."

"Good night." Silver closed the door, turned, and leaned her back against it.

Gracious! What could have made Whitney think such a thing? Silver felt no affection for Jared Newman. Certainly not of the romantic kind. Perhaps she'd begun to admire him a little after hearing the Hanovers' story. But that was all. Respect and admiration were as far as her feelings went.

Her dream rose up to mock her. She saw him seated on his pinto, felt his gaze turn upon her, wanted to—

Stop! It was absurd. And dreams meant nothing.

She would have to make sure no one else misinterpreted her feelings in the future. Most of all the bounty hunter himself.

Chapter 15

As they approached Green River City three days after departing Laramie, Silver felt relief when Jared told her they would get a couple of rooms for the night. Not so much because she would enjoy sleeping in a real bed again—although she would—but because it would give her some time by herself. It seemed that she couldn't look at Jared without Whitney Hanover's voice echoing in her memory: "You must love him a great deal . . . I saw it on your face at supper. It was there whenever you looked at him."

Love him? How could she love him? She barely knew him. Jared was little more than a stranger to her. While they traveled, he rarely spoke, and it wasn't much different when they stopped to rest the horses during the day or to camp for the night. The man was private with his thoughts and his past. She'd learned more about him during their brief stay with the Hanovers than in all the other hours she'd spent with him put together.

Then there was that dream. The one that lingered in her memory, day after day.

"Sometimes the heart understands far more than the mind, and much sooner too."

Perhaps Whitney was right. But the Bible, as her father was wont to remind her, said the heart was deceitful above all things. She'd best remember that. She'd made a bad enough mistake when she'd ignored her head's warning about Bob Cassidy, a liar, scoundrel, and thief. She didn't want to make an even worse one with a bounty hunter.

"There it is," Jared said as he reined in on the crest of a hill. "Green River City."

Embarrassed by where her thoughts had taken her once again, she followed the direction of his gaze and found the small town nestled beside the green-colored river from which it took its name. In unison they nudged their horses and started down the hillside.

Green River was much like other western towns built along the Union Pacific rail line. There was one main street bordered by a mercantile, a restaurant, a church, two saloons, the jail and county offices, a doctor's office, and a small hotel advertising clean beds and hot baths. Dust rose up in small clouds behind horses and wagons, turning everything the same dull shade of taupe.

The pair dismounted in front of the hotel, Jared's spurs jingling as he stepped onto the boardwalk. "You get us a couple of rooms." He squinted at the afternoon sun. "I'll take the horses to the livery stable and then check around town, see if I can learn anything. I'll meet you at the restaurant across the street at six o'clock." He took money from his pocket and offered it to her. "Can you wait that long to eat?"

Taking the coins, she nodded, thankful her stomach didn't growl and make a liar out of her.

"Here." He stepped off the boardwalk and removed the saddlebags from both of their horses. "You'd better take these with you." He dropped them onto her outstretched arm. "I'll take care of the rest of our things. See you at six." He led the horses down the street.

As she watched him go, his long, easy gait familiar to her, a strange feeling shivered up her spine. A feeling she couldn't define—and wasn't sure she even wanted to try.

The man at the railroad station was certain no one meeting Bob Cassidy's description had broken his trip at Green River over the past two weeks. "Truth be told, ain't been nobody get off the train but folks who live here for a good month."

The news didn't surprise Jared. Green River wasn't much more than a way station, a quick stop on the way to or from bigger cities west of Wyoming. Places like Virginia City, Nevada, where he believed the man with the scar was headed.

He felt that now-familiar twinge of guilt, knowing his questions about Bob Cassidy and Matt Carlton were more of an afterthought. If Jared ever learned those two were headed away from Nevada, he would abandon any thought of bringing in Silver's runaway fiancé.

Former fiancé.

He thought back to the meal he and Silver had shared with Tom and Whitney. He'd been uncomfortable with the Hanovers' words of praise as they'd told Silver what brought the three of them together. A man of honor, Tom had called him. A man who wanted justice above all else. It wasn't very honorable to make Silver believe that finding Cassidy was his top priority. As for justice? It might be what he'd sought for Tom, but it had little to do with his hunt for the man with the scar.

Revenge was what he wanted. Stone-cold revenge.

He headed back toward the hotel, planning to clean up before meeting Silver at the restaurant. But as he walked past the saloon nearest the train station, he glanced through the window and caught sight of another familiar face.

It had been a good six months, probably closer to eight or ten, since his path had last crossed with Doug Gordon's. The Pinkerton detective was based out of Washington, DC, but his work often brought him west of the Mississippi.

Jared pushed open the swinging door of the saloon and walked inside. Doug looked up from his cards as Jared passed by the table, but there wasn't even the faintest glimmer of welcome. Yet Jared knew in his gut that Doug had seen and recognized him. Which meant the detective was on the job. Fine. Jared could wait.

At the bar, he ordered his usual sarsaparilla, then turned and leaned his back against the counter. There weren't many customers in the dimly lit, musty-smelling saloon. Two men sat at a table closest to the doorway with glasses of beer in their hands. The only other occupied table held Doug with two card players and a dealer.

About five minutes later, Doug won the pot in the center of the table. One of the other men rose, grumbling, and left the saloon. Jared took his half-empty glass and carried it to the table. "Mind if I join you?" His fingers touched the back of the recently vacated chair.

"Not at all," Doug answered.

"My name's Jared Newman." He pulled out the chair and sat down.

"Jess Stone."

That confirmed Jared's suspicions. Doug was working. He didn't want anyone at the table to know his real identity or occupation.

Jared glanced toward the other player.

"Perkins," the man said, sounding less than friendly.

The dealer said, "Five-card stud," and began shuffling the cards.

Jared turned back to Doug. "Are you from around these parts, Mr. Stone?"

"I'm here to look at some property, but I'll be returning to the East soon. And you?"

"Arrived today. Headed for Virginia City, Nevada."

The dealer put cards, facedown, before each player.

"And what takes you there?"

Jared shrugged. "A hunch that I might get lucky."

"My mother told me a man had to make his own luck." Doug tossed his ante into the center of the table.

"So I've heard."

Silver checked the watch pinned to her bodice. It was six thirty and still no sign of Jared. He'd left her cooling her heels once again. It made her feel frustrated and angry and a little bit lost. Exasperating man! Well, she wasn't going to wait for him all night. She was starved half to death.

Looking about, she motioned for the waitress and placed her order. When her food arrived, she ate, but without enjoyment. Not even the berry pie, which had sounded so good as she read the menu, could brighten her spirits.

Jared was the cause. As usual. Such a difficult man to understand. There were moments when he treated her with kindness, when she caught a glimpse of a gentleman, but then the silence would return. Oh, the unyielding silence. Of course, she didn't truly care if she understood him or not, but some pleasant conversations might make the journey seem less long. Not to mention giving her less time to dwell in her own overactive imagination.

She checked her watch again. Where was he? Had he run into trouble of some kind? A bounty hunter must know any number of nefarious characters, some of whom could be in Green River City. He could be lying in a pool of blood somewhere, for all she knew.

No. That was her imagination at work again. If he were hurt, she would hear about it. News such as that would sweep through Green River as quickly as gossip did in Twin Springs.

But what if he hadn't taken the horses to the livery? What if he'd ridden out of town and left her behind? Although he hadn't threatened in recent days to send her back to her parents, he didn't like having her along. He'd made that clear enough. At best, he tolerated her presence. He might decide to leave her.

Silver paid for her meal and left the restaurant.

Outside, she saw about half a dozen horses tied up outside the saloons and heard tinny piano music playing from one of the establishments. Otherwise the town was quiet as the mantle of evening settled over it. Silver hurried along the boardwalk toward the livery stable at the far end of the street.

"He wouldn't just leave me here. He might not be as friendly as I'd like, but the Hanovers think he's an honorable man. An honorable man wouldn't desert a woman in a strange town with little money." Her attempt to convince herself died in her throat when she entered the livery. A lantern hung from a post, casting a yellowish light onto the hard-packed dirt floor. “Hello?” she called.

No one answered, but a horse snorted its objection at her sudden intrusion. Another nickered. A third pawed at the straw on the floor of its stall.

Silver moved past each enclosure, looking for the familiar pinto, sorrel, and buckskin. She found Jared’s horse in the far corner. At the sight of her, the gelding thrust his head over the stall door. Letting out a sigh of relief, she stroked his muzzle. “I knew I was being silly.”

The horse bobbed his head as if in agreement.

Silver turned and spied her mare and the packhorse in another, larger stall across the way. The last of the tension drained from her shoulders. Jared hadn’t left her. Perhaps it was time she began to trust him and stop being afraid.

Jared leaned back in his chair and glanced once more at the cards in his hand. A moment later he pushed a chip across the green felt surface, his gaze shifting toward the man across from him.

“I’ll see you.” Doug Gordon added another chip to those in the center of the table.

Jared laid down his cards. “Full house.”

“You’ve had a stretch of luck, Newman.”

"Tonight, at any rate." He pulled the winnings toward him.

Doug looked at the dealer. "I'm finished for the night." He turned toward Jared again. "I see you're not a hard-drinking man, but may I buy you another one of those?" He pointed toward the empty glass at Jared's elbow.

Jared shrugged. "If you like."

They rose in unison and walked toward the far end of the bar, where Doug ordered two more drinks. Neither spoke until the bartender had set the beverages in front of them and departed.

Softly, Doug said, "I could use your help."

Jared nodded as he turned his back to the bar and leaned against it.

"I expect someone to arrive by train in a day or two, if he isn't here already. My superiors in Washington are anxious to talk with this man regarding some confidential documents that are missing."

"Why Green River?"

"He's got family on a ranch south of town. I plan to ride out there tomorrow and have a look around." Doug paused, seeming to want a response. When he didn't get one, he added, "There'd be some money in it for you, Jared. Enough to buy a train ticket to Nevada."

That wasn't a lot of money, but it was more than he had now. At least he could be thankful he'd more than broken even while playing cards.

"But more money than you have, right?" Doug said, reading his thoughts.

Jared shrugged. "I'll need enough for two tickets. And for three horses." The words served as a reminder. He'd left Silver sitting in that restaurant for a long time. She'd probably given up and gone to the hotel by now. She'd be angry with him—and rightly so.

"Two tickets?"

"Yes. Someone's riding with me."

"Do I know him?"

"No, you don't. Miss Matlock hired me to find someone for her."

"You're traveling with a *woman?*" Doug's eyes widened.

"Yes."

"A *Miss* Matlock?"

"Yes."

"Hard to believe."

"For me as well. Now, what about that help you wanted?"

Doug took the hint. "I've let it be known around town that I'm looking to invest in a ranch and that I plan to ride out and have a look at different properties tomorrow. But there's one ranch in particular I need to see, and if the man I'm after is there, I need to bring him back with me. Are you willing to come along? There could be trouble. I doubt the man I seek will come along willingly."

If it meant being able to take the train the rest of the way to Virginia City, if it meant getting there in a couple of days instead of a matter of weeks, Jared was more than willing. "I'll join you."

"Meet me at the livery at noon tomorrow."

Jared pushed back from the bar. "I'll be there."

Chapter 16

Full darkness had fallen upon the town while Silver tarried inside the livery, and no light spilled through windows at that end of town. As she followed the boardwalk, she had to watch her step lest she trip and fall.

"Well, hello there." A man stepped from a break between buildings, blocking her path. "What're you doin' out all by your lonesome, little lady?" Lights from buildings down the street formed a pale outline around the beefy, broad-shouldered man.

Without answering, she moved to step around him.

He was quicker than expected and grabbed her by the arm. "That ain't polite, miss. Not answerin' me." He pulled her toward him.

His grasp tightened, and fear replaced irritation. Would anyone hear her if she cried out for help?

"Maybe you and me could spend a little time together." He brought his face closer, enough that she could feel his breath—stinking of alcohol and unwashed teeth—upon her skin.

"Unhand me, sir."

He chuckled.

"Unhand me or I shall have you arrested." She tried to jerk free.

He only held on tighter. Then she felt the cool tip of a knife press against her throat, ending her struggle.

"I think you'd better come with me, missy. Real quiet like."

Her knees went weak. She wanted to scream, but the sound lodged in her throat.

"We'll go back into the livery barn there."

She heard footsteps a second before she saw another man's approach. Something about the way he moved, even in the darkness, told her who it was. "Jared!"

Her assailant spun around but didn't release her.

"Silver?"

The next moment she was shoved to the ground, landing hard on her side. Pain shot from her elbow up to her neck as she heard the sound of knuckles connecting with flesh and bone. Grunts. Heavy breaths. The shadowy forms of the two men as they grappled above her. She pushed herself away from them and scrambled to her feet.

And then she heard a groan, different than the sounds that had come before. One man—Jared, she knew by his slighter build—stumbled back, bent forward at the waist. The other, her heavier assailant, turned and ran.

"Jared?"

"Yeah." His voice was soft, strained. "What were you doing out here in the dark?" He straightened. "You were supposed to meet me at the restaurant." He exhaled a breath.

"I did go to the restaurant. When you never came back, I decided to check on the horses. I was looking for you. I thought you'd left me."

"Who was that man?"

"I don't know. He came out of nowhere. I was walking back to the hotel, and suddenly he was in front of me. He grabbed me and wouldn't let go."

Jared stepped closer. "Did he hurt you?"

"No." But as she answered, she remembered the knife pressed to her throat, and icy tentacles of fear closed around her heart. She shivered. Shuddered violently and couldn't seem to stop. If Jared hadn't come upon her when—

With one arm he pulled her close to his chest. "It's okay," he whispered. "It's okay now . . . He's gone . . . It's okay."

She leaned into him, seeking safety in his embrace, grateful for his presence. They stayed like that, standing in the darkness, for a long while.

Only after Silver's shivering subsided did

Jared release his hold and take a step back. "You sure you aren't hurt?"

"I'm sure. You came in time."

"Then we'd better get back to the hotel." He turned to face the town, his hand at the small of her back, and began to walk, guiding her along beside him.

She felt the warmth of his hand through her blouse. The sensation was both comforting and disconcerting, and she had a sudden longing to get to her room, throw herself onto the bed, and give in to a storm of tears. Determined she wouldn't let her fear show again until then, she quickened her pace.

It wasn't until they were in the hotel and had climbed the stairs to the second floor that Jared released another sound. This time a strangled groan. She looked at him. His face had a strange gray pallor, and his free hand was pressed against his side.

"Jared, what's the matter?"

"Get me into my room. Quick."

She saw then that his shirt and hand were bloodied. "You're hurt. He stabbed you. Why didn't you tell me?"

"Just get me to my room."

She reached into the pocket of her skirt and found the two keys, one for his room, one for hers. At the end of the hall, she struggled to put the right key into the lock. She had to bear more of his weight as he weakened. Any moment now, he might crumple to the floor.

At last the key turned, and she pushed the door open before them. It took effort, but she managed to help him to the bed. With a gasp, he dropped onto the mattress and lay there, eyes closed, blood oozing through the fingers pressed against his side.

Jared heard Silver's voice from above him. "I'll send someone for the doctor."

"No. I don't want a doctor." He forced his eyes open. "Turn up the lamp and get me some water and a towel." He slid himself up the length of the bed until he could lean his back against the headboard.

He'd been hurt worse than this through the years and had developed a sixth sense about wounds. This one wasn't life threatening, but he did need to stop the bleeding before it drained more of his strength.

While Silver went to get the requested water and towel, he removed his shirt to have a look. The knife had made a clean entry and withdrawal, and it wasn't a deep wound. It could so easily have gone a different way. The assailant had had a good forty pounds on Jared. Instead of running away, he could have finished the job, both with Jared . . . and with Silver.

Memories of his sister as she lay dying flashed

in his mind. What if the same thing had happened to Silver? What if the man who'd assaulted her had succeeded? Even the possibility that it could have happened sickened him.

Silver returned to the bedside, holding the washbowl filled with water and a towel draped over her arm. When her gaze went to his side, her face paled a little. "I still say you need a doctor."

"No doctor. It would take money we don't have." He lifted his hand. "It's not as bad as you think. All it needs is a few stitches and a bandage. Are my saddlebags in here?"

"Yes."

"I've got needles and thread in one of them. In a small pouch." He chuckled at the look of surprise that crossed her face, then winced at the pain it caused. "You think a man can't sew? When you live like I do, you have to be able to do your own mending."

For a moment, he thought she might smile, but her expression turned grim instead. "You're going to want me to do this mending, aren't you?"

"Yes."

"I was afraid of that."

Silver had to concentrate to keep her hand from shaking as she inserted the needle into Jared's side. He never made a sound, even though she knew each stitch had to hurt. She didn't lift her gaze to see if she was right. Better to keep working. Better not to think too much.

But there was another reason she didn't look up—embarrassment. Her cheeks were hot with it. Never before had she seen a man's bare chest or well-muscled abdomen. It felt strangely intimate to be in Jared's hotel room, seated on his bed, her left hand on his skin while her right drew the thread through his flesh, closing the wound. Of course, there was nothing intimate about the situation. She was nothing more than a nurse to an injured man. But still . . .

When the last stitch was done, she tied it off and cut the thread with a small pair of scissors. As she set the articles on the stand beside the bed, she heard Jared release a long breath.

"Thank you, Silver."

She looked at him. His eyes had closed, and his face looked even paler than it had been earlier. "Is there anything else I can do for you, Mr. Newman?" *Jared.*

"No. I'll be fine." He paused and grimaced. "A night's sleep will put me right."

She didn't think one night would be enough.

"Go on to bed, Silver. I'll see you in the morning."

Chapter 17

There was a part of Jared that would have liked to take matters into his own hands when it came to the man who'd tried to hurt Silver. But when he got up the next morning, he dressed and went straight to the sheriff's office. After introducing himself and naming a couple of the better-known officers of the law he knew, he described the events of the previous evening.

"Gotta be Bill Winters or his brother, Mike," Sheriff Hinkley said after hearing the assailant's physical description. "More than likely Bill. He's the bigger of the two. More bear than man. Mean cusses, the pair of them."

As if in answer, the wound in Jared's side gave a sharp twinge.

"Is the little lady all right?"

"She wasn't hurt. Just scared."

The sheriff pointed in the general direction of Jared's wound. "Did you see the doc for that?"

"I'm fine. Just needed a few stitches." He shifted his weight from one foot to the other. "Are you going to arrest him?"

"If I bring Bill Winters in and you can identify him, then I'll arrest him for sure." He stood.

"I'm going with you," Jared said.

"Not sure that's a good idea, Mr. Newman.

That ride might open up those stitches you got holding you together."

"I've ridden in worse condition than this."

The sheriff stood. "Then I reckon we best get going."

Less than an hour later, Jared and Sheriff Hinkley brought their horses to a halt at the top of a rise. Up ahead Jared saw the small house that belonged to the Winters brothers, according to his companion. The surrounding terrain was rolling and treeless, and the small patch of plowed earth seemed good for growing little more than weeds. About twenty or so yards from the house was a lean-to that served as a barn. A large gray horse stood in a nearby corral, head low, tail swatting flies. A saddle hung over the top rail of the enclosure.

Calling this place a farm would stretch the truth beyond belief.

His gaze returned to the ramshackle house. One horse and one saddle might mean only one of the brothers was at home.

There was a pen at the far corner of the house, close to the corral, and it looked to him like it held several sleeping hounds. The instant they caught wind of the two men and their horses, they would send up an alarm. As if hearing Jared's thoughts, one of the dogs sat up and began to howl. In almost perfect unison, Jared and the sheriff yanked their weapons from the scabbards on their saddles and dismounted, taking cover in a nearby gully. A moment later, Jared saw the barrel of a rifle appear through the now-open door.

"You're on private land," a man called.

"Bill Winters, it's Sheriff Hinkley. I need to talk to you."

"What about?"

"About last night."

There was a moment's hesitation. "Don't know what you mean."

"Yes, you do. I'm referring to the young woman you threatened with a knife near the livery stables."

Silence, then the report of a rifle sounded an instant before a bullet struck the ground a few feet in front of Jared's position.

Sheriff Hinkley looked over the rim of the gully. "Bill, you don't want to do this. Be reason-a ble. Put down your weapon and come on out."

Another shot was fired, and this time it caught the sheriff in the right shoulder. The man gasped in disbelief as he dropped to the ground with a hard thud. "I should've known he'd do that," he ground out through clenched teeth.

"Stay put," Jared said. "I'll take care of him."

"Keep an eye out for the brother."

With a nod, Jared began to snake his way north along the gully, rocks and thorns poking him as he went. He feared he'd torn loose a few of Silver's carefully made stitches. She wouldn't be happy about that.

Silver was descending the stairs when she heard a man say, "Jared Newman's room, please." She stopped to study the stranger at the front desk.

"He ain't in," the clerk replied. "Rode out early this mornin'."

"You're sure?"

The same question echoed in Silver's head. She'd knocked on Jared's door a short while before. No answer. She'd assumed he was asleep. But it seemed he was gone. Ridden off somewhere without her. Again. Leaving her behind. Again.

"I'm sure," the hotel clerk said. "I saw him and the sheriff ride out of town together."

The stranger frowned. "Was there a lady with him?"

"No, sir. Just the two men." The clerk's gaze moved toward the stairs. "Is she who you mean?" He motioned with his head.

The stranger turned. After a moment, he removed his hat. "Miss Matlock, I presume."

Silver didn't like that he knew her name when she didn't know his. It put her at a disadvantage.

"I'm a . . . an acquaintance of Mr. Newman's. May we talk privately?" He motioned toward the restaurant across the street. "Perhaps over breakfast."

She wasn't sure what to do. He hadn't given his name, hadn't said how he knew Jared or knew her name. After last night she was feeling a bit skittish about strangers.

He moved toward the staircase, stopping at the bottom step. In a low voice meant only for her ears, he said, "My name is Doug Gordon. I work for the Pinkerton Detective Agency."

He didn't look dangerous or threatening. He wore a black suit over a white shirt. His dark hair was clean, his face pleasant. He had the look of a banker or a lawyer, not a criminal.

"I expected to meet up with Jared this morning. We made the arrangements last night. That's when he told me you were riding with him."

Deciding she could trust him at least enough to sit with him in a public restaurant, Silver descended the last of the steps. They left the hotel side by side and crossed the street. Neither of them spoke until they'd been seated at the same table where Silver had eaten her dinner alone the night before.

It was Mr. Gordon who broke the silence. "Did something happen last night? Was there trouble of some sort?"

She shook her head.

Doug raised a quizzical eyebrow. "I think you'd better tell me the truth, Miss Matlock. There must be a reason Jared rode out of town with the sheriff."

How much should she tell him? He might be Jared's friend, but he was still a stranger to her.

He sat back in his chair. "Let's see if I can reassure you. My name, again, is Doug Gordon. I'm a Pinkerton detective, and I've had occasion to work with Jared in the past. Mr. Newman is assisting you in finding someone. That's what he does. Finds people who need to be found. He hails from Kentucky but has not lived there in many years. Not since his family was murdered."

Murdered? She'd known they were dead. But murdered? Jared had left that detail out.

"You and he are on your way to Virginia City, Nevada, but your available funds do not allow you to travel by train. Which is where I come in. Jared was to meet me to help with a job that could have earned him your train fare. Only he didn't show up at the appointed time. That isn't like him." Doug motioned with his head toward the hotel. "Now it seems he rode out on a different mission without letting either of us know, so something changed between last night and this morning. Care to tell me what it was?"

The last of her reticence dissolved, and she quickly related the events of the previous night.

"How badly was Jared hurt?" Doug asked when she came to the end.

"He should have seen a doctor, but he refused to let me send for one. He asked me to . . . I stitched his wound instead."

Doug pushed back from the table. “I’d say they were going after a suspect. Only reason Jared would have gone along. And since he’s not in the best fighting shape, I think I’d better see if I can lend a hand. Hopefully the deputy can tell me where they went.”

Silver opened her mouth to say she would accompany him, then closed it without a word. Better to keep her thoughts to herself—after Doug Gordon was gone, she could do as she pleased.

Holding the rifle in front of him, Jared edged up the embankment. He could see the side and back of the house now, but there was a long stretch of barren ground between him and it. Too far for him to sprint across. His instincts told him Bill Winters knew where he was, even though the door was no longer in view. There was enough space between boards in the side of the place for someone to look out, even where there wasn’t a door or window.

He rolled onto his side and glanced down at his shirt. A red stain was spreading across the fabric, the blood warm and sticky against his skin. As suspected, he’d managed to rip open his wound. He lifted the shirt to check it out. Didn’t look too serious.

He returned to his stomach and inched up again, his gaze sweeping the area. There had to be a way for him to force Winters out. If he could just—

The horse in the corral lifted its head, its ears darting forward, its eyes set somewhere behind Jared. His body on full alert, Jared rolled onto his back and whipped the rifle into position. A split second later, a bullet whizzed by his ear. He returned fire.

The man who'd shot at Jared and missed—tall, beefy, undoubtedly the brother—stood no more than fifty feet away from him, a surprised expression on his face. His gun arm lowered, and the Colt dangled from his index finger before dropping to the ground. Then he staggered a step or two to the left before falling face forward into the dirt.

Jared flipped onto his stomach once again. "Give yourself up, Winters. You can either come willingly or go with me feet first."

A glimpse of Bill Winters's face appeared at the corner of the shack. "Mike?" he shouted.

"Your brother can't help you now."

A string of foul curses punctured the air.

Jared felt a moment of hope. Maybe Winters would recognize the futility and give himself up. But the hope died a second later when the dogs—five snarling hounds—shot around the corner of the shack with teeth bared, driven forward by a command from their master. Jared felled three of them in quick succession. Then the last two were upon him. He swung his rifle at the closest, knocking it away with the barrel. Even as he tightened his finger on the trigger, he felt teeth sink into his left forearm. In a reflex motion, he struck the animal on the head with the rifle stock. The dog fell away, stunned.

From the corner of his eye, he saw Bill Winters step into full view, but there was nothing he could do about him now as the last surviving dog lunged for him. Dropping the rifle—useless to him—he grabbed the canine and held him away from his neck. The pair of them, man and dog, rolled to the bottom of the gully.

He was out of luck. If the attack dog didn't rip his throat open first, Winters would shoot him soon enough. There it was. Gunfire. He waited for the impact of the bullet as it entered his body . . . but it didn't happen. He rolled with the dog in the opposite direction, feeling the strength draining out of him.

A second shot. Then a third.

A high-pitched yelp.

The dog dropped onto him, a deadweight on his chest.

Heart in her throat, Silver lowered the revolver to her side and ran toward Jared. She was vaguely aware of Doug Gordon kneeling beside the man who'd assaulted her the previous night, but all she cared to know was if Jared was all right.

"Jared?" she called as she drew closer. "Jared?"

There was a grunt, and the large dog's carcass rolled off of Jared.

She dropped to her knees beside him.

He scowled at her while he gripped his arm, blood seeping through his fingers. "I guess you weren't lying when you said you could shoot."

"Of course I wasn't lying."

"Did you shoot Winters too?"

She shook her head. "No. Mr. Gordon shot him. He's dead, I think." She motioned toward Jared's arm. "How badly are you hurt?"

"Not bad. But we need to get the sheriff back to town. He took a bullet in the shoulder. I left him up the gully a ways."

Doug Gordon's shadow fell across the two of them, and they both looked up.

"You shouldn't have let her come with you," Jared said.

"I didn't let her. She followed me."

Jared released a tight chuckle. "I should've known. Telling her to stay put is a waste of time."

When he looked at her again, Silver recognized the pain in his hazel eyes, but she saw something else too.

He was glad she was there.

Her heart skittered in response.

Chapter 18

The physician closed his black bag and looked at Jared where he lay on the bed in his hotel room. "You get some sleep, young man. You'll have plenty enough discomfort until those wounds heal. Dog bites can be nasty things, and rest is the best medicine for you now."

"I will, Doctor. Thank you."

With a nod in Doug's direction, the physician left.

Jared drew in a deep breath and let it out, thankful the laudanum had taken the edge off his pain. And thankful that, according to the doctor, the sheriff was going to be fine as well.

"I should go," Doug said, stepping closer to the bed. "I've got a train to catch."

"You're leaving Green River? What about your suspect?"

"He wasn't on his way here after all. I got word they arrested him up in Montana last night. I'm going there now."

Jared nodded. They wouldn't be taking the train to Virginia City after all.

"Sorry there's no reward," Doug said.

Jared gave a small shrug. "It's all right. Besides, I'm the one who owes you. If you hadn't shown up at the Winters's place when you did . . ."

"Me and Miss Matlock, you mean."

"Yeah, you and Miss Matlock."

Doug stepped closer to the bed. "Wish I didn't have to leave, but I've got no choice. At least there won't be any trouble for you with the sheriff since he was there for the whole thing." He patted Jared's shoulder. "You take care. And I hope you find what you're looking for in Virginia City."

"Thanks."

"But do yourself a favor. Stay put for a couple days like the doctor said."

"I don't think I'll have any choice."

Doug placed his gray bowler over his dark hair. "One more thing, my friend. Take care of Miss Matlock."

"I'll try."

"I have a feeling there could be something special between you two, if you'd give it a chance." He turned and walked toward the door. "I like her, Jared. She could change your life for the better." And with that, the door closed behind Doug.

Something between him and Silver? That's what Tom Hanover had thought too. And now Doug. Why? Because Silver had risked her life and ended up saving his? Had she done it because she cared or because she needed him to find Bob Cassidy and the money he stole? Whatever the answer, it didn't matter to him anyway.

As his eyelids drifted closed, his thoughts returned to Fair Acres, back to a time of butter-sunshine days, colts racing through green pastures, mint juleps served in the shade of the veranda. And on that veranda . . . Silver Matlock, her black hair cascading about her shoulders like a waterfall.

Crazy.

Beyond crazy.

It had to be the laudanum . . .

Balancing a tray with one hand, Silver rapped on Jared's door. When he didn't answer, she opened it and looked inside. He appeared to be asleep, as the physician said he should be. She started to close the door.

"You can come in, Miss Matlock."

She pushed the door open farther. "I didn't mean to wake you."

"You didn't. I'm just a bit groggy." He pushed himself up against the pillows at his back, grimacing as he did so. "What time is it?"

"Almost five." She stepped into the room and closed the door behind her. "I thought you might be hungry. I've brought some soup and bread from the restaurant."

"I could eat. Thanks."

She carried the tray to the bed and set it on his lap, then turned to leave.

"Don't go." When she looked at him again, he

motioned with his head toward a nearby chair. “Stay and keep me company.”

The invitation relieved her. She’d wanted to stay. She’d needed to see how he was doing. There hadn’t been a moment all day that he hadn’t been in her thoughts, that she hadn’t recalled the sight of him in that ditch, his shirt torn and bloodied. He’d sworn to her it looked worse than it was, but she needed to see that for herself.

Jared picked up the spoon from the tray and dipped it into the bowl. “You talk while I eat.”

“Talk about what?” She sank onto the chair.

“Anything you want. Tell me about your life in Twin Springs.”

“We’ve been over that before.”

“Not really. Is that where you were born?”

“No.” She shook her head. “My father owned a store in Ohio before bringing us to Colorado. I was seven when we moved. I remember it was both exciting and scary, leaving everybody we knew behind. My stepmother didn’t want to move, but once we settled in Twin Springs and the mercantile began to succeed, she seemed happy enough. There were lots of miners going through town back then because of so many gold strikes up in the mountains. Mother was certain we would be as rich as Solomon himself. She was determined we would one day move to Denver and become part of grand society. What she wanted most in the world was for my sister, Rose, to marry someone of wealth and position." She smiled at the memory of her stepsister's wedding, how happy Rose had been as she married the man she loved—a man with little money and no position in the society Silver's stepmother coveted. But at least Rose and Dan Downing lived in Denver. That was some consolation for Marlene Matlock.

"What about you?" Jared asked. "What sort of man did she envision for you?"

Silver laughed, though it was bittersweet. "I doubt she ever had much hope of me marrying well, if at all. I was a skinny, gawky child, more interested in books and horses than boys. That didn't change much as I got older. I have few feminine qualities to my credit. She fears I will wind up a spinster."

"Surely you didn't believe that."

"That I would be a spinster?" She shrugged. "Yes, I did think it. I do think it. Not many men approve of my radical thinking."

"What sort of radical thinking?" Jared slid the tray from his lap to the bedside stand.

"You should eat some more of that."

"I've had enough for now. What sort of radical thinking?"

His persistence surprised her. Or maybe it was his interest. "Like women voting. Why shouldn't we enjoy the same right as men? We're citizens of this country too. Who knows? Given the vote, we might one day see a woman president."

Jared loved the sparkle in her eyes, the excitement in her voice. While he doubted there would ever come a time that a woman occupied the White House, he couldn't help but enjoy listening to Silver talk about such a possibility.

"Would you want to be president?" he asked.

"Me? Heavens, no."

"What about a senator or governor?"

Her smile broadened as she shook her head. "Not those either. I've listened to my father often enough to know I haven't the patience for politics. But some women will serve in those positions someday."

"So what would you want to do, if there was nothing to hold you back? Not people or money or anything else. Freedom to do whatever you most wanted."

"I'd own a ranch. A horse ranch. Maybe a little like the place your family had. I would raise the best stock in all of Colorado. Maybe I'd go to college so I could think like a businessman. And I suppose, if I could, I would travel to places I've only read about. Like Europe or the Far East."

"Miss Matlock, I believe you could do all of that."

She stiffened and her smile disappeared. "Are you laughing at me?"

"Not at all. I meant it."

There was a lengthy silence before her shoulders rose and fell on a sigh. "Well, I suppose you should laugh. It does sound preposterous. Even to me."

"Is that why you agreed to marry Mr. Cassidy? Because you couldn't have what you really wanted?" He regretted the words. The question was unkind—and the answer none of his business.

She turned her gaze toward the window. "Yes, I suppose that was the real reason. Although I didn't realize it at the time."

He hadn't expected a reply, let alone one in the affirmative.

She squared her shoulders as she faced him again. "If you're finished eating, I should take the tray and go. The doctor wants you to get lots of rest."

"Stay a little longer, Miss Matlock. Please. I didn't mean to offend you."

"I wasn't offended. How could I be?"

"Then stay," he repeated, surprised by how much he wanted her to comply. He was used to solitude and in many ways preferred it. Just not this time.

A frown pinched her forehead. "All right. For a short while. But only if you tell me more about yourself. Enough has been said about me."

"I never have been comfortable talking about

myself." He almost regretted asking her to stay.

"I know that you grew up on a Kentucky horse farm, that your father and grandfather raised racing stock, and that you have no living family members." Her voice softened. "Tell me about them. About your family."

Something about the tone of her voice and the kindness of her eyes made him willing to answer her questions. "I was sixteen when we got the news that my brothers had died in the same battle. I wanted to join up after that, but my father wouldn't let me, even though boys younger than me were going off to fight for the Confederacy. He claimed he needed me to help run the farm, but with most of the horses gone, I knew it wasn't the truth. He just didn't want to risk losing another son on the battlefield. I understand better now, but I was angry with him at the time."

He pictured his brothers as they'd once been, a fun-loving, mischief-making pair. They'd taught him to hunt and fish and swim. They'd also taught him how to stand up for what he believed and to do his best, no matter what.

With a shake of his head, he continued, "It wasn't easy holding on to Fair Acres after the war. Taxes were high, and without breeding stock we didn't have a way to bring in revenue." He shrugged. "Even if we'd had horses, there weren't many who could afford to buy them."

"I'm sorry. It must have been difficult for all of you."

"My little sister, Katrina, was the one who kept us going. She was full of sparkle and life. Never complained about anything." He looked at the woman seated beside him. "She was a bit like you."

Silver's disbelief was obvious in her expression.

"Katrina was too young to remember what Fair Acres had been like before the war, but my father swore it would be great again. He would see that his only daughter had the best of everything. Dresses and parties and—" He broke off as the pleasant memories turned dark, as he'd known they would.

"What happened, Mr. Newman? Why did you leave Fair Acres?"

A familiar coldness washed over him. "My family was murdered."

She hesitated, and he saw the understanding in her eyes. "You weren't there when it happened, were you?"

"No. Maybe if I had been . . ." He closed his eyes, feeling the hatred well up in him again. He would find the man with the scar who'd battered his little sister and left her to die. He would find the man who'd killed his parents. If it took him the rest of his life, he would find him and exact his revenge.

• • •

Silence gripped the hotel room. Jared's face was a rigid mask. Silver guessed he was remembering the grim details of the day he discovered his family. A part of her wished he would share them with her. The other part was relieved he kept them to himself.

"It took Katrina three weeks to die." He looked at Silver, his eyes gone cold. "I will find the man who killed her."

"That's why you became a bounty hunter."

"I'll find him, no matter how long it takes."

Looking at him, she saw the boy who'd been raised in comfort, in the bosom of a loving family. She saw the son who'd wanted to fight in the war but had been kept safe at home. She saw the heartsick young man who'd buried his parents and sister. She saw the seeds of bitterness that had been born out of that tragedy. She saw the man who'd been shaped by long days in the saddle, long nights beneath the stars, following fugitives from the law, seeking vengeance on the one who'd taken everything from him.

She saw Jared, the boy he'd been, the bounty hunter he'd become, and the man he still could be. And as crazy as it was, she knew she'd begun to love all three.

Chapter 19

They left Green River two days later. By this time, Silver knew Jared wasn't one to dawdle on the trail. If he was in pain from his injuries, he didn't allow it to slow them down. He would have kept going until they both dropped dead in their tracks if it weren't for the horses. The animals he took pity on, but not himself or Silver.

Three days of riding carried them across the border into the territory of Utah. As if trying to drive them back to Wyoming, the winds blew and the skies wept upon them for another three days. Huge thunderheads with black underbellies roiled overhead. From dawn to dusk, cold water ran in rivulets over their slickers, and they bent their hats into the wind to protect their faces from the stinging rain. It soaked through their boots, drenching their socks. Each night they sought dry shelter with little success.

At noon on the last day of the storm, they spied a break in the clouds on the western horizon. The wind widened the strip of blue until, by evening, the sun prepared to set with nothing but an azure expanse above it.

Silver slid from the saddle, then turned and rested her forehead against Cinder's neck, weariness overwhelming her. How she longed for dry clothes and a soft mattress. She'd reached the limit of her endurance. She'd thought she was up for the task, but maybe she'd been wrong.

"I'll gather some firewood," Jared said, "while you tether the horses."

She glanced over her shoulder, but he hadn't waited for her acquiescence. At least he'd found them a good campsite. It was set against a rocky butte. The wall of stone would protect them from wind and weather, and thankfully the soil beneath her boots was hard and dry. No mud to contend with for a change.

It wasn't long before Jared returned and built a fire. Then, while Silver prepared their supper, he sat on a large rock and checked their dwindling supplies. His activity allowed Silver to watch him with unguarded eyes.

Her feelings hadn't altered since the evening in Green River—the night he'd shared about his sister and she'd realized she was falling in love with him. But what future could be found with a bounty hunter, a man without home or roots? Even if he was interested in her, which he wasn't. He only cared about the reward she offered. He wasn't unkind, but she knew he merely tolerated her presence. He would be glad when they found Bob and he could send her back to her home in Twin Springs.

But it didn't feel like it was her home. Not anymore. And if she didn't retrieve the money

Bob had stolen, her parents wouldn't have a home either.

If only . . .

Jared looked up from the pack saddle, and their gazes met and held. Her pulse skipped. What if he should read what she felt in her eyes? She didn't want that. It would be too embarrassing. She'd already proven that her head and heart were not to be trusted.

Lowering her gaze, she reached for the coffeepot and poured the black brew into a cup. "Would you like some?" She held the tin cup out to him. "It's ready."

"Fit to drink?" It wasn't the first time he'd teased her with that question. He always asked it with the hint of a grin, as if they shared a private joke.

"It's every bit as good as yours." She tried to sound insulted but knew she failed.

He stood, stepped forward, and accepted the cup from her hand, taking a sip. "You're right." He grinned. "It is as good as mine. Better, I think."

"I doubt that."

He hunkered down close to the fire, resting his backside on his boot heels. "We ought to sleep better tonight."

"Dry ground will be a nice change."

"Yes." He took another sip of coffee. "Our supplies are getting low. We need to make up some of the ground we lost in the bad weather."

"I noticed we aren't following the railroad tracks any longer."

"This is a shortcut." Jared glanced west. "We'll rejoin the line by tomorrow night. I doubt Cassidy and Carlton would have any reason to stop in Mormon territory. No gambling here."

Silver held out a tin plate toward Jared. "The beans should be hot by now."

He took the plate and covered it with a mess of beans, then moved a short distance from the fire and settled onto the large rock again. Silver dished up her own supper, glad for a hot meal, even if it was just beans from a can.

"The next stretch will be a long and hard one," Jared added after more silence. "There isn't much between here and Nevada besides sand."

Silver stifled a groan. If what came ahead was harder than what they'd already endured, she didn't know how she'd make it. Then again, quitting wasn't an option.

Jared woke in the middle of the night. A breeze rustled the trees, turning them into swaying black skeletons, visible in the light of a quarter moon. The air was pungent. A mixture of pine and damp earth. The nearby creek gurgled as it spilled out of the steep crag bordering the trail.

Alert, he listened for a sound that shouldn't be there. Something beyond the normal sounds of night. He heard nothing out of the ordinary.

Neither too much noise nor too much silence. Reassured, he relaxed.

He rolled onto his side and stared across the campsite. Moonlight had found Silver's face. In repose, the strain of the journey had disappeared. Her chest rose and fell in a gentle rhythm. Peaceful. And seeing her peace, he felt some of it spill over onto him.

He'd always preferred to ride alone, to work alone. He was comfortable with his own company, with quiet and solitude. But these past few weeks, he'd become used to having Silver with him. He was starting to like having someone to talk to around the campfire as he ate his dinner. No. That wasn't the whole truth. He was starting to like having *Silver* there to talk to.

A dangerous admission.

Chapter 20

Mile after miserable mile passed beneath the horses' hooves. The icy rains that had drenched them to the skin became fond memories beneath a relentless sun. The dust rose up in billowing clouds to blind their eyes and choke their parched throats. The high-country desert crested and dipped in never-ending waves before and behind them. Always in the distance, there seemed to be the promise of some cool oasis, but it never materialized. Jared and Silver pushed onward with steely resolve.

It was midafternoon when they saw the small homestead with its windmill. Hoping for some cool well water, they rode toward the weather-beaten house and barn.

The first shot hit the ground in front of Silver's mare. The second just missed Jared's ear. An instant later, Jared threw himself against Silver, knocking her from Cinder's back. The horses bolted, trotting away in the opposite direction, reins dragging on the ground. Jared searched for better cover. Then he grabbed Silver's upper arm, pulled her to her feet, and ran, half towing, half dragging her with him toward some thick sagebrush.

"Hello in the house!" he shouted. "We don't want trouble. We're thirsty. We just need water and we'll be on our way."

In response, another bullet hit the dirt.

"It seems to me you get shot at a lot," Silver said.

"Sometimes it seems that way to me too." Jared peered over the silver-green sagebrush that sheltered them. The door stood open a crack, and he saw the barrel of a rifle sticking out. Silver was right. It was all too similar to what had happened outside of Green River City.

Turning his head, he confirmed his horse had gone too far away to retrieve his rifle without being exposed to more gunfire. He would have to make do with his revolvers. He lowered himself again, and his gaze turned upon Silver. "We've got to have water. We can't stay trapped here all day. Think you can cover me?"

"Of course I can cover you. I've done it before, haven't I?"

Good. He'd irritated her. He would rather have her mad than scared. He removed the gun from the left holster and handed it to her. "Stay put and keep under cover." He drew his remaining Colt from the right holster, checking the chambers out of habit, although he knew they were full. Then he started to move away.

"Jared . . ."

He glanced back at her.

"Be careful."

This wasn't the best moment to think how long it had been since a woman cared about his safety, so he shoved the thought away. Then, crouching forward, he sprinted toward another clump of sagebrush.

Darting from cover to cover, he made an arc toward the back of the house. Whoever was inside had to see him working his way around, but no more shots were fired. Was he headed for an ambush?

He reached the house and pressed himself against the board siding. Forcing his breathing to slow, he inched his way to the side and toward the front. When he poked his head around the front corner, he glanced toward Silver's hiding place. He could see the top of her ebony hair and wanted to yell at her to get down, but he didn't dare. The door was still open, the rifle barrel still visible. Sliding sideways, he moved toward the doorway. There was no sound from inside, no indication his presence might be suspected.

It was a chance, but he took it. He holstered his revolver and reached slowly toward the barrel poking through the opening. As his fingers closed around the metal, still warm from the shots fired earlier, he jerked upward and outward. Then he spun and kicked the door with his boot, knocking it open with a crash. In an instant he had the rifle turned on its owner.

The boy—and he was definitely a boy—had been knocked to the hard-packed dirt floor when the door flew open. He stared at Jared with a terrified expression. Jared made a quick survey of the room. The lad was alone, although the door to the back room of the house was closed.

"Stand up," Jared ordered.

The boy obeyed, brushing off the seat of his pants as he did so.

"Anyone else here?" He jerked the rifle barrel toward the closed door.

The boy shook his head.

"Why were you shooting at us?"

"I didn't know who you was."

"Where are your folks?"

The boy's expression seemed to crumple. He didn't cry, but he was close to it. "Dead."

Jared took hold of his arm and drew him outside into the daylight. "It's all right, Silver," he called. "Get the horses and come on in."

The boy was scrawny, maybe ten or eleven years old. His hair was a deep chestnut brown and in need of trimming. Dark brown eyes looked out from a dirt-smudged face.

"What's your name?"

Silver arrived at Jared's side. She glanced at the boy, then at Jared, then back at the boy. "Was he the one shooting at us?"

"Yes. Doesn't seem to like strangers. Says he's here alone and his folks are dead."

"Let go of him, Jared." She knelt before the boy. "He's terrified."

With a handkerchief drawn from the pocket of her skirt, Silver tried to wipe the dirt from the boy's face. "You must have a good reason for shooting at two complete strangers. Why don't you tell us what it is?"

The boy lost his fight against tears. They welled over and streaked his cheeks. "I thought . . . I thought he might be comin' back to kill me too."

Silver used the falling tears to wipe away a

little more of the dirt. "Who might be coming back? Who was killed?"

The boy hiccupped over a sob.

Silver put her arms around the boy and drew his head to her shoulder, her fingers stroking his hair. She waited in silence until the crying ceased. Then she drew back and met his gaze again. "My name is Miss Matlock, and this is Mr. Newman. We're on our way to Virginia City. We saw your windmill and were hoping to find some water." She stood, causing the boy to look up at her. "Now you know all about us. If you tell us your name, we won't be strangers any longer."

He sniffed and wiped his nose on his sleeve. "Dean."

"Dean what?"

"Dean Forest."

"And where are your parents, Dean?"

He jerked his head toward the room with the closed door. "In there. They . . . they're dead. They was killed this mornin'." He stuck out his chin, trying to look brave but failing. "Pa killed one of 'em. He's down over that rise there."

Jared turned in the direction of Dean's gaze. "There's a body over there?"

"Yessir."

It was Jared's turn to take a knee in front of the boy. "Dean, you need to tell us what happened."

"Me and Pa, we was comin' back with a lamb that wandered off. When we got close to the house, we heard Ma screamin' something awful. Pa made me go up in the loft of the barn and hide, then he went to help Ma. I reckon there was somebody inside and somebody outside. The one that was inside with Ma, he shot both of 'em dead."

Silver felt herself go cold. "You saw it?"

Dean shook his head. "No. I was hidin' in the loft, like I told ya. But I saw what he did when I come down."

"I'll need to get them buried," Jared said softly to Silver.

"I'll help you."

"You don't have to."

The last thing in the world Silver wanted to do was help bury this boy's parents or the outlaw who was dead somewhere behind her, but it had to be done. She refused to let Jared do it alone. They were equally hot, tired, and exhausted. "We'll get it done faster with two of us."

"Are you sure? It won't be pleasant."

"I'm sure."

Jared nodded as he put his hand on the boy's shoulder and looked down at him. There was great kindness in his voice when he said, "Show me where the shovel is, son."

Dean nodded as the tears started to fall again. Then the pair of them walked toward the barn.

Silver drew in a deep breath as she looked at the open door of the house. *Just get on with it. If that poor little boy could be in there with his dead parents, you can stand whatever you find.*

She tried to take a step forward, but she couldn't seem to make her foot move. It felt like the bottom of her boot was nailed to the ground.

All right, then. If she wasn't ready to go into the house, she could start with the hoodlum in the shallow ravine. He must have been an evil man to be part of this attack on an innocent family. She needn't feel the least remorse at his passing. There were a couple of blankets hanging on the line off to one side of the house. She would get one of them and wrap the body in it. Then Dean wouldn't have to see him again.

After retrieving the blanket, she moved toward the gully, her shoulders stiff, her steps slow but determined. She saw a black boot first. Then two of them. One leg lay at an odd angle. Next she saw the shirt and flesh covered in blood, turned almost black by this time. She had to stop for a moment to steel herself again before taking the final step that brought her to the edge of the rise. The man's head came into view, his face turned partially away from her. She was thankful for that. She didn't think she—

He groaned.

A small shriek escaped her lips, and she covered her mouth with one hand. He wasn't dead!

His eyes opened, glazed with pain, not seeming to see her.

She took another tentative step toward the man, and only then did she recognize him. "Bob?"

She began to shake. Shake so hard her knees wouldn't hold her. She dropped to the ground.

Bob groaned again. "Water," he whispered between dry, cracked lips. "Please."

She'd found him. He was gut shot and dying, from the look of him, but she had found him. The search was over.

"Water."

Silver pushed herself to her feet again and hurried to the pump, where she filled a bucket with water and returned as quickly as possible. When she offered Bob a drink with the ladle, he took hold of her hand with both of his, guiding the bowl of the ladle to his lips. She wanted to jerk away from his touch, but a shred of compassion kept her from doing so.

"Thanks," he mumbled, his head dropping back to the ground, eyes closed.

"Bob, what happened here?"

He looked at her again, and this time he seemed to see her. His eyes widened in shock. "Silver?"

"Yes, it's me."

He stared at her. "How did you find me?"

"It doesn't matter. What matters is, do you have the money you took from Father? Do you have Mother's jewels?"

"Carlton . . . Is he dead?"

Silver shook her head. "He's gone. We didn't

see him. It looks like he killed the man and woman who lived here."

He made a sound that was half laugh, half groan. "And then he . . . left me to die too. Without a . . . a backward glance. Just . . . like him."

"Maybe we can get a doctor. Maybe—"

"No use. I'm . . . done for."

Was it completely callous, even heartless to ask a dying man a second time about the money? Though it felt like it, she did it anyway. "The money, Bob. Do you have it?"

He coughed, choked, pressed a hand against the wound in his belly. At last, in a raspy voice, he answered. "What was left of it . . . was in my . . . saddlebags. If . . . if Carlton's gone, so's . . . the money."

Hope wrestled with despair. Not all the money was gone, which was good news, but whatever money and jewels were left were now with a man she didn't know on his way to a destination she didn't know either. A man who had killed a young boy's parents and left his friend to die in the heat of the sun.

Jared's voice intruded on her thoughts. "Silver?"

She turned and watched his approach.

"What are you—" He broke off suddenly as his gaze fell on the man beside her.

Silver stood. "It's Bob," she whispered. "He's alive."

"Bob? You mean Bob Cassidy?"

She nodded. "He needs a doctor."

Jared knelt beside Bob and examined the wound. When he looked up, he shook his head, silently telling her no doctor could make a difference. She'd known it already.

"Should we try to carry him inside? It's so hot out here."

Before Jared could answer her question, a soft sigh escaped Bob's lips and his right hand slid from his belly to the ground at his side. There was no corresponding intake of air.

Bob Cassidy, the man she'd once meant to marry, was dead.

Jared saw how shaken Silver was, and he wondered if she harbored stronger feelings for Mr. Cassidy than she'd admitted to him. Or maybe it was the shock of thinking she would find a body down in this shallow ravine and instead finding Bob Cassidy, still breathing. Whatever the reason for her fragile state, he thought it best for her to rest awhile. He would tend to the bodies without her help.

He drew her up and escorted her to the barn. He expected some resistance when he told her to sit in the shade and not move until he told her to. For a change, she didn't argue. Jared called for the boy and asked him to stay with Silver.

It took time for Jared to dig three graves on

one side of the barn where the ground was softer. The graves weren't deep, but they were deep enough. And with each shovelful of dirt he threw out of the holes, his thoughts churned.

It was nothing short of a miracle that their path had crossed with Bob Cassidy's. Jared hadn't thought they would ever find the man. Not in his wildest dreams had he believed it was possible. He hadn't even been looking for Cassidy and Carlton. All he'd been focused on was getting to Virginia City and finding the murderer of his family.

Stumbling upon Cassidy had left Jared with plenty of questions too. Where and why had Bob Cassidy and Matt Carlton gotten off the train? What had caused the man called Carlton to kill Dean's parents? This was obviously a poor homestead. It couldn't have been for money.

More important, what should Jared do with the boy when he and Silver moved on? How far were they from the next town? What would Silver want to do now that her search for Bob Cassidy was over?

Pausing over that one, Jared admitted to himself he would miss her if she went back to Twin Springs. All those times he'd wished he could be rid of her, all those times he'd threatened to do just that, and now he hoped she would stay. Hoped she would continue on with him a little longer. The discovery surprised him, as few things did.

Finally, the graves were ready. Jared leaned the shovel against the barn and went for the first body. He wrapped Bob in the blanket that Silver must have dropped. Then he lifted the body and slung it over his shoulder, carrying the dead man to the prepared burial plot.

Then it was time to take care of the boy's parents. Jared made sure Silver and Dean were still sitting in the shade. They were. He headed for the house. He found the boy's father face-down on the floor of the bedroom, just inside the doorway. Jared stepped over the body and glanced toward the bed. In an instant, he went cold all over.

The woman's hair had been shorn. Like Katrina's. Like Felicity's. Like all the other victims' he'd come across. And he knew. The man he'd sought all these years—the man without a name or solid description beyond a scar on his collarbone—was a gambler going by the name of Matt Carlton.

Everything inside of him screamed for him to run out, get on his horse, and ride like the wind after the killer. He was mere hours behind Carlton, but Carlton couldn't know that. He wouldn't be looking out for Jared. His defenses would be down. This was Jared's chance. The best one he'd ever had.

He drew a deep breath. As much as he wanted to, he couldn't do that to Silver. He couldn't ride out and leave her behind. Or the boy either. Nor could he keep this discovery to himself. Silver must be told. He'd kept enough things from her. It was time to put all his cards on the table.

With care, he wrapped Mrs. Forest in a blanket and carried her to one of the graves. He repeated the action with Mr. Forest. Then he shoveled the dirt back over the bodies. As if knowing the deed was done, Silver and Dean came around the corner of the barn, Silver holding the boy's hand.

Jared dropped the shovel. "We should get going. We have a lot of ground to cover. We need to take the boy to the sheriff in Elko."

"We should say something." Silver motioned toward the three graves. "We should pray for them."

"Prayers won't help them now."

"No, but they might help us," she answered softly.

That gave him pause. He looked to the boy and then back at Silver. He saw the understanding in her eyes, saw her acknowledge his hesitation and then silently ask him to join them anyway. Taking a breath, he nodded.

His mother had known her Bible forward and backward. Many of his memories were of her on her knees in prayer. He'd been there too. It shamed him, all of a sudden, how far astray he had wandered from the teachings of his youth.

Still holding Dean's hand, Silver closed her eyes and began to pray. What she said didn't matter much to Jared, didn't really penetrate his conscious thought. But something about the way she prayed brought light to a place inside Jared's chest that had been shut up in darkness for many years.

Chapter 21

After gathering Dean's belongings and adding what food was available that would travel well to their stores, they put Dean on the packhorse and headed west again.

That night, after Dean had fallen asleep, Jared asked Silver to step away from the campfire so they might talk in private. She expected he was about to suggest she get on the train at the earliest opportunity and return to Colorado. Bob Cassidy was dead, and Matt Carlton had taken what was left of her father's money and jewels. What were her chances of finding him when she didn't know him? Slim at best.

But that wasn't what Jared had to say to her. Instead he told her everything he now knew about Matt Carlton, and the horror of his story made her forget to be angry with him for lying to her.

"I don't know why Carlton and Cassidy got off the train," Jared said. "They should've been in Virginia City already. Maybe Carlton just wanted to kill again. Doesn't matter, really. I've got a name. I'll find him now. I'll bring him to justice. See him hang."

Of course. Why hadn't she thought of it before? It was so obvious. "There's a reward offered for his capture, isn't there?"

"Possibly. Several years back, the husband of one of Carlton's victims in Texas told me he'd pay handsomely if I brought his wife's killer to justice. But I've been out of touch with Mr. Harrison a long time now. He may not even live in Texas any longer. There's no guarantee of collecting a bounty."

"But there's a chance."

Jared nodded. "A chance. Why?"

"I'm going to help you find and bring him in."

He immediately stiffened. "No."

"You wouldn't know who he is if it wasn't for me. *I'm* the reason you were tracking Bob Cassidy, and *Bob* is the reason you know about Matt Carlton. I deserve some of that reward."

Jared scowled. "It's too dangerous. Weren't you listening? Didn't I explain well enough what Carlton did to those women?"

"It's no more dangerous now than when we didn't know who he was. We were still tracking him, even if you didn't know it."

"Maybe it isn't more dangerous, but it feels like it."

"I won't be sent back, Jared. I have to continue on. I have to, for my father's sake."

He stared at her in silence for a long time before saying, "We'd better get some sleep. We can talk about this more after we see the sheriff in Elko."

Silver moved toward her bedroll without further argument. He wouldn't change her mind, no matter what he said. She would stay with Jared. She would help bring in Matt Carlton. She would collect part of the reward, if there was one, and if not, at least she might recover some of the money and jewelry.

Jared hadn't known anyone who could frustrate and confuse him the way Silver Matlock could. He would have to be crazy to let her continue on with him. It wasn't good for anybody, letting her get to him the way she did. He needed to focus on finding and capturing Matt Carlton. That needed to be his only concern.

"You're goin' after the man who killed my ma and pa, aren't ya?"

Jared swiveled on the heel of his boot.

Dean Forest stood a few feet away. "I heard you talkin' to the lady. You know who done it, and you're goin' after him."

He decided the boy deserved the truth every bit as much as Silver had. "I've been on his trail for a long time. He's killed before."

"You the law?"

"No."

"Bounty hunter?"

Jared nodded.

"I'm goin' with ya."

"Sorry, son. I've got my hands full as it is."

"I ain't your son." Dean stepped forward, his hands balled into fists at his sides. "And I ain't stayin' in Elko. You leave me there, I'll come after you on my own. I gotta right t' see him swing for what he done."

It was a little like seeing himself. He hadn't been as young as Dean when he'd found his family murdered, but he recognized the emotions in the boy's dark eyes. He recognized the desire for revenge, the need for justice. He'd felt it all before. He'd been living with it for years.

"Maybe you do have that right," he replied, "but you're not going along."

The boy shot him one more angry look, then turned away. "You just try'n stop me."

Chapter 22

Silver held on to Dean's hand as Jared talked to the Elko sheriff.

The man, with grizzled jaw and stringy hair, leaned back in his chair. "I reckon Lucas Feldt would take the boy in. He's got himself a mighty big ranch and can always use a hand with the chores. His missus is kinda sickly and not much help around the place no more. Don't know how long he'd be willing to keep him, though." He rubbed the day-old whiskers on his chin. "How'd you say you come by him, Mr. Newman?"

"His folks died," Jared answered. "We found him all alone on their small farm."

"Where you say you're headed?"

"I didn't."

The sheriff eyed the double holsters. "Don't wanna tell me, huh? You got any reason for that?"

"Don't mind telling you. We're headed for Virginia City."

The sheriff's gaze shifted to Silver, then to Dean. "Mighty hot crossin' on horseback. Most folks take the train these days. You and the missus oughta think about takin' the next train through." He leaned forward, placing his elbows on his desk. "How'd your folks die, boy?"

Dean shook his head.

"Can't you talk?" When Dean didn't reply, the sheriff looked at Jared again. "Not gonna be easy finding anyone to take in a dumb mute. Even Lucas Feldt's not likely t' want him if'n he can't talk."

Silver bristled. She'd like to give the man a piece of her mind.

"Why don't you folks take yourselves over to

Maddie's across the street. She sets out a right good meal. I'll check around an' see what I can come up with for the boy. He don't look too strong. Kinda thin, if you ask me. And if he don't talk . . ." He shook his head.

Silver clasped Dean's hand all the harder as she pulled him with her outside. Another second in there, and she would have given in to her temper.

As soon as Jared joined them on the boardwalk, she turned on him. "You can't mean to leave Dean with that horrid man or anyone he could find. They'd just be looking for a spare field hand. Hasn't he been through enough?"

Squinting, Jared looked up at the noon sun. He rocked back on his heels, then rolled forward again. Finally, he glanced down at Dean. "You still mean to try to follow us if we leave here without you?"

The boy nodded.

"Then I suppose we're wasting time talking to the sheriff. You can stay with us for now. Just remember, it's temporary."

Silver sensed the decision hadn't been easy for Jared. But his heart was tender enough for him to agree with her, and it made her want to hug him. She resisted the urge.

"Let's get something to eat and be on our way," Jared said. "The sooner we get to Virginia City, the sooner this will be over."

• • •

I must be out of my mind.

It wasn't the first time Jared had thought he was a fool, and it probably wouldn't be the last. Especially now. Not only had he been traveling with a woman while trailing a cold-blooded killer, but now he'd taken on a scrawny, frightened kid.

They ate a quick and inexpensive meal at the restaurant, then rode their horses, Dean back on the packhorse, to the train station.

Jared stepped up to the ticket window. "I'm looking for a man who might've caught a train west in the last day or two. He's not from around here. Just passing through. Tall, dark blond hair, blue eyes. Have you seen him? It's important that I find him." He glanced through the open station doors where Silver and Dean waited on horseback, hoping the clerk would assume it was a family matter.

"Sorry. No strangers out of here this past week. Just local folks."

Jared tugged at his hat brim. "Thanks."

He didn't know if he was glad or not that Matt Carlton hadn't taken the train out of Elko. It could mean they were right behind him and had a chance to catch up with him. Or it might mean Virginia City was no longer his destination. If Carlton had taken off in another direction, they wouldn't know it, and the advantage would be lost.

But he was out of options. They would have to press on toward Virginia City and hope Carlton was headed there.

That night, while Silver and Dean slept on the opposite side of the campfire, Jared lay awake, staring up at the stars.

He was close. Closer than he'd ever been to finding the man who'd killed his parents and sister. God willing, he would find Matt Carlton in Virginia City. He would haul him back to Colorado where he could stand trial. It would be easier to prove his guilt there than anywhere. He could write to Owen Harrison in Fort Worth. Another person who could attest to Carlton's atrocities.

And then what? What would he do when he was no longer looking for the man with the crescent-shaped scar? Would he go on, just as before? Would he still be a bounty hunter? And if not, then what?

Utter weariness washed over him. He was bone tired. Soul tired. Tired of the endless miles. Tired of the dirt and the hunger and the heat. Tired of carrying a gun and always being ready to use it. Tired of the hate that ate at his soul. Tired of what he had become.

He used to dream of going back to Fair Acres, but that was impossible. Kentucky was a part of his past, a part he couldn't return to. His fingers touched the cool metal of his Colt revolver. Violence. That's what he knew. That was all he knew anymore. He'd become accustomed to it.

He looked across the campfire at Silver, and a longing stirred within him that had nothing to do with physical desire. He allowed it to linger only a moment before he drove it away.

Silver Matlock was too good for the likes of him. He would only end up hurting her by association.

Silver sensed Jared watching her. Her heart begged her to open her eyes and meet his gaze. Her head demanded she pretend to be asleep. The Good Book said the heart was deceitful above all things and desperately wicked. So she listened to her head. This time.

She rolled over, turning her back to the fire—and to Jared. Removing the temptation to look at him. For nearly a month, she'd traveled with him. He could be hard. He could be distant. But he could also be kind and gentle. She caught glimpses of the good in him every day. Had she really fallen in love with Jared Newman? How could she love him? He'd never kissed her, never encouraged her affection in any way. And yet . . .

Tears slipped from beneath her eyelids and dropped onto the rolled blanket beneath her head.

They would find Matt Carlton. She was certain they would. They would collect a reward—she was certain of that too—and she would be able to rescue her father from financial ruin. But then Jared would ride away, leaving her behind. And she could not bear thinking of that fast-approaching day.

Chapter 23

It was around noon, three days after leaving Elko, as their small party rode along a narrow trail on a hillside, the sun overhead as scorching as ever.

All of a sudden, Cinder reared up, her shrill whinny jarring the silence that had accompanied them for miles. Unprepared, Silver tumbled into the draw below, slamming hard at the bottom. Agony exploded in her head and the wind was driven from her chest. Shards of pain shot up her leg.

From a distance, she heard Jared say, "Don't move." But then he touched her, and she realized he was beside her. How had he reached her so quickly?

She opened her eyes and tried to sit up.

"I said don't move." He gently pushed her back.

She grimaced. "I'm all right."

"Sure you are." He began to explore her limbs with his hands.

When he reached her right ankle, she gasped in pain.

He frowned. “Better take your boot off and have a look.”

When he lifted her foot off the ground, a wave of dizziness sent her spiraling toward a black pit. She fought to remain conscious and dug her fingers into the dirt as he removed her boot.

“Wiggle your toes,” Jared said, still elevating her leg.

She managed to do so.

“It’s not broken. A bad sprain, I imagine. But you’re not going to get that boot back on. Look how swollen it is already.” He lowered her leg to the ground. “Dean, you’d better bring the horses down. We’ll camp here for the night.”

The boy nodded—she hadn’t noticed that he was down in this ravine as well—and took off at a run.

“We ought to make Winnemucca by tomorrow night. We can have a doctor look at your ankle there.”

“We can’t afford a doctor. I’ll be all right.” She remembered Jared saying something similar after he’d been knifed and almost smiled, despite the pain.

Jared grunted. “We’ll see how you feel about that in the morning. For now, we’d better try to make you comfortable.”

“What made her spook? It happened so fast, I didn’t see anything.”

"A rattler."

"Where's Cinder now?" Silver twisted and tried to look up the steep incline. Her head throbbed in response to the sudden movement.

"Not sure. She ran off a ways." He looked up the hillside. "I'd better help Dean. Will you be all right until we get back with the horses?"

"Yes."

"I'd try to make you more comfortable, but—" He lifted empty hands.

"I'm fine where I am. Just go before Cinder runs off too far."

Jared rose above her. "We won't be long."

As soon as he was out of sight, Silver released the groan she'd been holding in. The pain was worse than she'd let on.

Tears burned the back of her eyes. Why did this have to happen on top of everything else? She had less than sixty days left to find Matt Carlton and get the reward and save her parents. There was no time to be laid up with another injury, hers this time. Their supplies had dwindled to almost nothing. They had little money left for any purpose, let alone to pay for the services of a doctor.

It all suddenly seemed hopeless.

Jared knew Silver hurt more than she let on during the final leg of their journey to Winnemucca, but she didn't complain. Not even once.

Though they could ill afford it, Jared used some of their precious remaining coins to pay for a hotel room. If they had to stay long, they would soon be completely broke and hungry.

After paying for the hotel room, Jared returned to the street and helped Silver from her horse, never letting her feet touch the ground. He carried her into the lobby and up the stairs. The three-week-old knife wound twinged a bit from the effort, but he ignored it.

They reached the door to the room, and without him asking her to, Silver reached out, turned the knob, and pushed the door open. The room was small but clean, the bed covered with a patch-work quilt, the window hidden behind bleached muslin curtains. There was an oval rag rug in shades of blue on the floor. A cherrywood dresser with a mirror stood against one wall, a wash-stand with pitcher and bowl against another.

As Jared set Silver on the bed, he said, "I only had enough to pay for one room. Dean and I can sleep on the floor."

She nodded without comment.

"I'm going to check around town, see about a doctor."

Silver touched his wrist before he could step away from the bed. "Wait, Jared."

She reached beneath the neck of her bodice and withdrew the locket. In the weeks they'd been together, he'd seen her touch or hold it numerous times as they sat near the campfires. As if she drew comfort from it. No one had to tell him it was precious to her.

"Take this and sell it. Don't let anybody cheat you. It's valuable. That's a real diamond. The necklace belonged to my great-grandmother, who left it to my mother when she died, and my mother left it to me. But don't use the money you get for a doctor. We need other things more. My ankle is sprained. That's all. I'll be able to ride hard and fast again in a couple of days."

He took the proffered necklace, feeling like a failure as he did so. He'd let her ride along with him. He should be able to take better care of her.

"All right," he agreed. "We'll see how you feel in the morning." He turned toward the boy. "Dean, come with me. We'll bring in our supplies, and then I'll take the horses to the livery."

Half an hour later, Jared stepped out of the livery stables and glanced down the dusty main street. He removed his hat, wiping his sleeve across his forehead, then replaced it with a firm tug. As he'd done in every town since Laramie, he would start with a few questions at the train station.

Winnemucca had begun as a trading post, but it had grown into a fair-sized town with the coming of the railroad. It had the typical false-fronted stores and saloons, most of them unpainted, all of them faded by the hot desert sun and cold winter winds. The main street was wide to facilitate turning wagons. Jared had passed through a hundred towns like it in the past six years.

The clerk behind the counter at the rail station looked up from beneath his green visor. “Can I help you, sir?”

Jared described Carlton with a few words.

“Not much to go on. Can’t say as I’ve seen him, but doesn’t mean he didn’t come through here. Hey, your name wouldn’t be Newman, would it?”

Jared tensed. “Yes. Why?”

“Got me a telegram here for you.” He handed Jared an envelope.

“Thanks.” He turned away as he ripped the seal and pulled out the telegram. It was from Doug Gordon.

He went back and read the contents. *Three murders . . . Suspect in jail in Silver City, Idaho . . . Could be the man you’re looking for . . .*

Carlton in jail in Idaho? Could it be him?

Jared turned toward the clerk again. “Does the stage to Idaho come through here?”

“Sure does. San Francisco to Boise City and vicey versey.”

“Where can I find the schedule?”

“You’re in luck if you’re headed north. Next one through’d be ’round six o’clock tonight. Passengers board across the street.”

“Thanks.”

He went outside, pausing on the boardwalk. His gaze moved to the hotel while he shoved his hand into his pocket, fingering the few remaining coins and the locket Silver had given to him. The stage—with a change of horses every ten to fifteen miles—would be a good four days faster than if he traveled by horseback, but he didn't have enough money on him at the moment to pay the fare. He would have to get it somehow. He *had* to get there and back fast. If it was Matt Carlton sitting in that jail, Jared's search would be over. He could start his life over again. Somewhere. Somehow. Maybe with someone by his side.

Maybe with Silver by his side.

Silver. If he told her face-to-face about the telegram, she would want to go too. She would insist on it. No, better to force her to wait for him to come back. Call him a coward, but he would rather send her a note, along with enough money to keep her and Dean until he returned from Silver City. He ought to be able to get enough for the packhorse to take care of those expenses. The locket he would hold on to. Despite her generosity in offering it, he wasn't going to sell it. Not yet, anyway.

Silver grew worried when Jared didn't return to the hotel after several hours. Finally, she sent Dean to look for him. The waiting was pure agony. She wanted to *do* something. Lowering her legs to the floor, she tried to stand, but her ankle couldn't support her. She dropped back onto the bed with a small cry as pain shot up her leg.

As if in answer, the door opened and Dean stepped into the room. "Couldn't find Mr. Newman anywhere." He looked at her foot where it rested on the floor, then glanced down at his own feet, his hands shoved into the pockets of his overalls. "Cinder an' the pinto are in the livery, but the man there said he bought the packhorse I was ridin'."

"Jared sold the packhorse? But why would he—"

"Fella said he seen Mr. Newman get on the stage."

"The stage?" It wasn't possible. He wouldn't leave them there. She used to fear he might do that, but not anymore. The information had to be wrong. Jared wouldn't take the money from her necklace and the sale of the packhorse and desert them.

"I asked at the express office. He's gone, all right."

The betrayal burned hot in her stomach. She swallowed back the rising panic and tried to think logically. He hadn't sold his saddle horse along with the pack animal. He had to be coming back. But where had he gone, and why had he left without telling her? How long would he be away? If he was headed for somewhere close by, he would have ridden there, not bought a ticket on the stage.

He's abandoned us. He wants the reward money all to himself.

After all this time, after all those miles, he'd left without a word or a backward glance. In the beginning, she would have thought him capable of it. But not now. Not after he'd won her trust . . . and her heart.

And yet he'd done it.

She drew her injured ankle up from the floor, propping it high with an extra pillow and blanket. She forced her voice to sound calm. "Let's get some sleep, Dean. We'll worry about what to do in the morning. If you're hungry, there ought to be something left to eat in the saddlebags."

"I ain't hungry."

Jared had betrayed the boy too. Dean had believed Jared would find and capture the man who'd killed his parents. Now what?

She closed her eyes. *Lord, please help me to know what to do next. Help me take care of Dean too. Give me strength to do this alone.*

Alone. She didn't want to be alone, but that's where she'd found herself once again.

The stage bounced and rocked on its leather springs, jerking its inhabitants from side to side. Holding on to the side panel of the coach, Jared stared out the window. The setting sun cast a reddish hue across the desert floor, making the sage look like bushes of fire.

Jared wondered how Silver had taken the news of his going. No, he didn't wonder. He knew. She would be angry that he'd left her and Dean behind. She wanted to be a part of the capture of Matt Carlton. She would have declared herself able to take this journey. And that would have led to an argument. He didn't want to argue with her. Not ever.

Maybe he shouldn't have entrusted the note of explanation and the remainder of the money from the sale of his horse to the Wells, Fargo agent. But that's what those agents did. They delivered mail and gold all over the West. Why not down the street to the hotel?

Yes, she'd be angry with him today, but hopefully she'd be over it by the time he returned. And if he came back with the news of Matt Carlton's capture, all the better.

Jared leaned back and drew his hat brim down low, hoping to get some shut-eye.

Chapter 24

Leaning on Dean, Silver entered the livery stable. She waited a moment for her eyes to become accustomed to the dim light. At the back of the building, she saw the red glow of a fire and heard the roar of a bellows and the clang of metal as the blacksmith pounded an iron shoe against the anvil. She and Dean moved slowly in that direction.

"Excuse me, sir," she called, but her voice was drowned out by the noise. The smithy hammered away. "Excuse me," she hollered a second time.

Still no reaction.

She reached out and touched the man's shoulder.

He startled. Swearing a blue streak, he turned toward her with his hammer raised. He lowered it when he saw her. "What're you doin', sneakin' up on a man like that?"

"I'm sorry. I called to you, but you didn't hear me."

He gave an abrupt nod. "What can I do for you?"

"I . . ." She tried not to think about what she was about to do. It hurt too much. "I understand you buy horses."

"Sometimes. If I like what I see." He set aside his hammer, then wiped his hands against his leather apron. "What you got?" The man's face was darkened by soot and reddened from the heat of the fire. He was about the same height as Silver but would have tipped the scales at more than double her own weight. His eyes seemed rather small in his large, square face, showing entirely too much white around them. She hated the idea of selling Cinder to him, but she had no other choice.

She turned toward the stall that held her horse. "The buckskin mare. She's mine. I'd like to sell her if you're interested."

"She's yours?" he asked, his tone suspicious.

Silver straightened and tried to speak with authority. "I was traveling with Mr. Newman, who brought in three horses. He sold you the sorrel gelding yesterday, correct? Did he sell you the pinto as well?"

"Might have done. What business is it of yours if'n he did?"

"None at all." The answer stung her heart. "But the buckskin is mine, and I should like to discuss a fair price for her."

The blacksmith drew his arm beneath his nose as he sniffed. "She'd be a good mount for a woman, I reckon." He moved toward the stall.

"Yes, she is." Silver followed him, still leaning on Dean. "She's a good saddle horse for anyone. Man or woman. And she's strong, with plenty of endurance. She's carried me all the way from Colorado."

"Hmm."

"If you don't want her, I'll ask around town."

"Don't get your nose in the air, little lady. I never said I wouldn't buy the mare."

We should be headed for Colorado. I shouldn't be doing this on my own.

Silver and Dean stepped from the station

platform onto the westbound train. Using the money she'd obtained from the blacksmith for Cinder, she'd purchased two tickets for Carson City, where they would change passage from the Central Pacific Railroad to the Virginia & Truckee Railroad for the final leg of their journey.

But what would they do when they got there? Heaven only knew. She knew nothing about finding a fugitive from the law. But she hadn't made it all the way from Twin Springs, Colorado, to Winnemucca, Nevada, just to turn around empty-handed. Jared Newman may have deserted her—it felt even worse than when Bob left her at the altar—but she wasn't letting him claim any reward alone. She wanted and needed it, and she had some right to it. Jared owed her a share.

She plopped down onto the seat in the passenger coach. Hard as a rock. At least the trip wasn't long. Her ankle throbbed too, but she'd put up with worse over the last month.

As for Jared, she hoped he was miserable, wherever he was by now.

Dean shoved the saddlebags beneath the seat, then sat opposite her. It might not have been the best thing, bringing him with her, but she wouldn't leave him behind the way Jared had left her. Dean belonged with her now. Whatever came, he belonged with her.

The boy squinted at her. "You doin' okay, Miss Silver?"

"I'm fine, Dean. Thank you."

Please, God, take care of us. Keep us from danger. And have mercy upon my family. Please let there be a reward or enough of Father's money left.

Jared stepped out of the Silver City jail. He was disappointed but not surprised to find the prisoner and suspect of three murders wasn't Matt Carlton. The man had, indeed, fit the physical description, but he didn't have the distinctive scar, nor had he been in Colorado in recent months. Jared had confirmed all of that with the sheriff. The man had been right there in Idaho for the past year.

Jared placed his hat on his head, then stepped off the boardwalk and started across the street toward the hotel, hoping to find something to eat and a cheap room for the night. The southbound stage wouldn't be through Silver City until the next afternoon. The wait would be intolerable, especially because his coming had been in vain.

As he ate, his thoughts drifted to Silver. Had she forgiven him by now, seen the wisdom in his decision to come to Silver City without her? When she got mad, she turned as cold and unyielding as an iceberg in the Arctic. Luckily for him, she usually thawed before giving him a piece of her mind. Her impulsive nature could get her into trouble too. She needed someone to keep that impulsiveness in check.

She needs me *to keep it in check.*

But did she really need him? She deserved someone better than a bounty hunter. He had nothing to offer her, even after they caught up with Matt Carlton. If they caught up with him.

Reality was the guns strapped to Jared's thighs and days spent in the saddle as he chased one fugitive from the law after another. It wasn't the gray-eyed beauty from Colorado. He'd best remember it.

Chapter 25

Helplessness washed over Silver as she gazed along the main street of Virginia City. She hadn't imagined the town would be this big. A continuous line of roofs stretched for a distance of five miles—or so she'd been told—and more spread out on either side, rising up the mountain on her right and downward on her left. Thirty thousand people lived in Virginia City and its sister city of Gold Hill. Thirty thousand souls hoping to get rich, one way or another. Dust filled the air as horses and wagons moved along the thoroughfares. The sun baked the arid mountain terrain, scorching the flowers planted by women trying to bring a little color to this corner of the world.

How on earth would she find Matt Carlton in such a place? Assuming he'd come here at all. There were dozens of saloons and gambling dens and nearly as many hotels. It would take her days to search out each. Perhaps Jared had already found him. Perhaps Jared was somewhere in Virginia City right now, counting his reward.

She thought of the small stash of money she possessed. How long would it last? The prices she'd seen in store windows were exorbitantly high. If she turned around now, perhaps she would have enough to purchase two tickets to Colorado. But only if she did it right away.

A wagon lumbered past them, and Silver's gaze was caught by the stoop-shouldered man holding the reins. His bald head was bare, his expression one of defeat. A woman, her face dour and bleak, sat beside him on the seat. The wagon bed was piled high with what Silver assumed was all they had left to call their own.

She thought of her parents being thrown out of their home. Where would they go? What would they do? Would they wind up someplace like this with no money and no hope? She couldn't let that happen to them, no matter what she had to go through. She couldn't back out now.

She grasped Dean's hand within her own. "We'd better find a place to stay."

Three doors down, they entered the lobby of

the Banner Hotel. Silver walked up to the counter, nerves making her throat dry.

"Sir," she said to the clerk, "how much for a room?"

"Haven't got any empty ones. Whole town's like that." He eyed her over his glasses, and a smile tugged at the corners of his mouth. "Got me a storeroom I can put a couple of cots in. I'd let you have it for five dollars."

"Per week?"

"Per night."

She felt her eyes widen. "But that's robbery."

He shrugged. "Maybe so. Take it or leave it."

"Is there a boardinghouse nearby? A respectable boardinghouse."

The clerk barked a laugh. "If that's what you're looking for, you come to the wrong town, missy."

Her stomach now tied in knots, Silver drew Dean outside again.

"Where we goin' now?" the boy asked.

"We'll keep looking. There has to be someplace we can afford to stay for a few nights."

Half an hour and five hotels later, Silver continued to lead Dean along the boardwalk, despair giving way to panic. She was tired, hungry, and terribly afraid. How could they afford anything in this town?

As they approached a dressmaking shop, sandwiched between a dry goods store and a drugstore, a buxom woman carrying a parasol stepped through the doorway onto the boardwalk. The lavender parasol with its white lace edging hid the woman's face from view, but it was the gown that captured Silver's attention. It had been a long time since she'd seen anything so lovely.

The violet silk dress had a trained skirt trimmed with four scalloped flounces, each surmounted by a band of black velvet ribbon. The overskirt and waist were a lighter shade of violet faille with white lace and black velvet ribbons and bows. The sleeves were long with lacy cuffs, and the woman's hands were covered with matching gloves. She looked dressed for an audience with a king, not a day of shopping in a dry and dusty town like Virginia City.

The woman turned toward Silver as she switched the parasol to her other shoulder. Silver's breath caught, the lovely dress forgotten. The woman had the face of an angel, every angle perfection. She might be twenty; she might be thirty-five or older. She appeared timeless.

The woman's light blue eyes were friendly as she met Silver's gaze. She inclined her head slightly. "Good day."

How embarrassing to be caught staring. "Hello," Silver whispered in response.

"You look lost. May I help you find something? Or someone?"

Silver remembered the string of hotels behind her and blurted out, "We're looking for a place to stay. Someplace affordable. My funds are limited."

Soft laughter escaped the woman's cherry-pink lips. "There is little affordable in Virginia City." She held out a gloved hand. "My name is Corinne Duvall."

"I'm Silver Matlock." She shook the woman's hand and felt the roughness of her fingers catch on the delicate fabric of the other's glove. "And this is Dean."

"How do you do, sir." Corinne shook the boy's hand before her eyes shifted back to Silver. "How long do you intend to stay in Virginia City, Mrs. Matlock?"

"I . . . I'm not sure . . . And it's Miss Matlock."

"Ah. I see."

Silver flushed as she realized what the other woman thought. "Dean is not my son. His parents died recently. I . . . I'm caring for him."

"Well, it would not have shocked me if he were your son, though you would have been a very young mother." Corinne's eyes narrowed thoughtfully. "If your funds are limited, I assume you'll be looking for suitable employment as well as a place to stay?"

"Yes . . . I . . . I suppose so." What had she thought? That she would waltz into Virginia City, capture Matt Carlton, collect a reward, and go home in style? As happened all too often, she'd acted without thinking through all of the possible consequences.

"Then perhaps I can be of some help. If you'll come with me, Miss Matlock." With a hand lifting the front of her skirt enough to reveal the toes of her violet walking shoes, Corinne Duvall led the way toward a buggy tied in front of the dry goods store. "Put your things in the back, Miss Matlock." She stepped into the buggy and took up the reins.

Silver hesitated, unsure what she should do. "Miss Duvall, we can't impose. We are strangers."

"My dear girl, Virginia City is filled with nothing but strangers. They come and they go all the time. I would have no friends at all if I waited until I knew someone well. I remember what it was like, arriving in town without knowing a soul. Besides, this street isn't the safest place for a beautiful woman to be, especially with evening approaching. Come along now. It's obvious your ankle bothers you, and you shouldn't be walking on it. Get in."

Feeling swept downriver by a strong current, Silver obeyed. As soon as Dean climbed into the back, Corinne slapped the reins against the horse's rump, sending the buggy rolling down the street.

Jared glared at the hotel clerk. "What do you mean, she's not here?"

"Just what I said. She paid her bill and left."

"Where did she go? When did she leave?"

"It's not my business, mister, to be askin' the

guests where they're going, but she checked out three days ago."

Jared swallowed his frustration. "Thanks." He turned toward the exit.

"Mister!"

He turned again.

"She left some things behind. Said they was yours if you came back. I put 'em in the storage room behind the kitchen." He pointed.

"Thanks," Jared repeated. "I'm going to the livery to get my horse. I'll be back for my things when I'm done."

He walked toward the livery stable. "Foolish, stubborn woman," he muttered beneath his breath. She'd probably left Winnemucca to give him a dose of his own medicine. It wasn't enough for her to wait for him as he'd told her in his note. No, she had to take the money and buy herself a train ticket out of here. And it didn't take much of an imagination to guess where she'd gone. He paused inside the barn doorway. "Mr. Crandon!"

The blacksmith stepped out of a stall, a pitchfork in hand. His eyes narrowed when he recognized Jared. "I wondered if you'd be comin' back."

"I told you I would return." He looked down the row of stalls on his left until he found the familiar black-and-white head poking over the rail. The pinto nickered. "You didn't think I'd leave my horses behind, did you?"

The smithy shrugged as he set aside the pitchfork. “I didn’t know what to think after that lady friend of yours come in and sold me her mare.”

“She what?”

“Sold me that mare o’ hers. She’s standing out back there. I got me a buyer comin’ by t’ look at her later.”

Jared had left Silver enough money to hold both her and the boy until he got back. She wouldn’t sell Cinder without a good reason. That horse meant a lot to her.

He stepped toward the blacksmith. “Did she say where she was going?”

“No, sir.”

Jared didn’t need anyone to tell him where she’d gone. He knew her well enough by now. Nor did he need anyone to tell him that she hadn’t received the money he’d left her. Only desperation would have caused her to sell the buckskin.

Jared pointed at the man. “Do not sell that horse. I’ll be back for it and my pinto.”

“I paid good money for it. Got a right to sell it if I want to.”

“You’ll have your money.” He turned on his heel and marched out of the stables.

Corinne Duvall’s palatial home sat on a hillside overlooking Virginia City. It was an enormous redbrick structure with white shutters at the windows and a veranda on three sides. Rosebushes twined around the narrow columns on either side of the front steps. Unlike elsewhere in this scruffy mining town, a skilled gardener had succeeded in producing colorful blooms and a patch of green lawn. The moment Corinne stopped the buggy, the front door opened and a short, slight man dressed all in black hurried toward them.

"Thank you, Chung," Corinne said as he helped her from the buggy. "Please take Miss Matlock's things to the blue room." She glanced toward Silver. "Come with me, dear."

Silver got down as instructed, then paused to stare at the three-story house before her. All she'd done was ask for directions to an inexpensive place to stay, and now she, a complete stranger, was invited to stay in this mansion. It was more than a little unusual.

Dean's hand gripped hers, causing her to look at him. Her own surprise was mirrored in his eyes. He'd probably never seen anything like this house. His home had been a shack on the high desert. He had to be even more overwhelmed by this than Silver.

She squeezed his fingers. "I guess we might as well go inside. I can't see that it will do any harm. Can you?"

Dean shook his head.

"All right. If nothing else, we can see if it's as fancy inside as out."

Chapter 26

Corinne Duvall waited for them in the entry hall. She leaned the handle of her parasol against the wall, a panel of violet silk balancing on the shiny parquet floor, then removed her gloves, laying them one on top of the other on the dark mahogany table near the front doors. Watching her reflection in the mirror above the table, she freed her bonnet and lifted it from her yellow curls.

"I love hats, but they can get tiresome," Corinne said, meeting Silver's eyes in the mirror. Then she waved a manicured hand toward an arched doorway. "Let's get comfortable, shall we, and you can tell me about yourself and why you've come to Virginia City."

Silver's hand tightened around Dean's as they followed the woman into a large parlor. There were fireplaces with elaborate screens at both ends of the room. To the right was a white grand piano, its curved edges trimmed with gold paint. A white fur rug lay beneath it. Several groupings of chairs were placed about the high-ceilinged room, and plenty of light spilled through the glass windows, their heavy brocade drapes pulled open and tied back.

Dominating everything else in the room, above

the far mantel, was an enormous portrait—at least fifteen feet high—of Corinne Duvall in a riding habit. Silver couldn't help staring at it.

"Quite good, isn't it? I believe the artist earned his commission."

Silver glanced over her shoulder toward Corinne.

"Maurice, the artist, was in love with me when he painted it. You can tell. He was kind to me."

"He wasn't kind. It looks just like you." Silver's gaze returned to the portrait.

"When I was younger, perhaps. No more."

Corinne Duvall was wrong. She was still as beautiful if not as young.

"Come, Miss Matlock. Join me." Silver turned to find Corinne now seated on a white-and-gold brocade sofa. She gestured toward a companion piece not far away. "Please sit down."

"Miss Duvall, I—"

"Everyone calls me Miss Corinne. Please do so. And will you allow me to call you Silver?"

"Of course. But I don't understand why you brought us to your home. All we wish is to find a place to stay that is clean and safe and that we can afford."

"Those are the very reasons I brought you home with me, my dear. Virginia City is not a safe place for an unaccompanied woman. Particularly not for one as attractive as you. If I'd left you in town, goodness knows what might have happened to you. We have more than our share of drunkards, outlaws, and cutthroats in Virginia City." Once again she motioned toward the nearby sofa. "Now, please sit and tell me about yourself."

Silver felt she had little choice but to obey.

Corinne smiled, prompting gently, "Where are you from?"

"A small town in Colorado, near Denver."

"And what brought you to Nevada?"

Silver hesitated. What should she say?

"A man?"

Yes, but not the way Corinne meant.

"When I came to Virginia City, I was a penniless orphan. To survive, I worked in a saloon and entertained the men. It wasn't a nice existence. But I was smart and I was lucky, and I managed to change my life for the better." Corinne's smile was fleeting. "There are many reasons why girls end up in a place like Virginia City. I try to keep as many as possible from going through what I went through."

Silver didn't understand Corinne's full meaning, and yet a shudder passed through her for the little she did comprehend.

The Chinese manservant appeared in the doorway carrying a silver tray.

"Ah, my afternoon tea." Corinne motioned him forward. "Thank you, Chung. You'll have some too, won't you, Silver? Such a civilized practice—tea in the afternoon."

The manservant set the tray on the low table between the sofas.

"Chung," Corinne said, "when we are finished with our tea, please show Miss Matlock to the blue room and draw her a bath. The boy should have the room at the end of the hall on the third floor. The one on the north side."

It seemed settled. Silver and Dean were staying. At least for one night. She could decide about what came next tomorrow.

Steam rose around Silver's face as she reclined in the porcelain tub. She hadn't felt anything this wonderful in a month of Sundays. A lazy glance took in the opulence of the bathing room with its ornate molding, gilded mirror, and multicolored bottles of sweet-smelling bath salts and perfumes.

Finally, with the water growing cool, Silver stepped from the bathtub and dried herself with a plush towel. She wrapped her hair in a second towel. It would still be damp when she went down to supper, but she didn't care. It was clean, and she felt renewed because of it. Even her ankle seemed better because of the bath.

The bedroom she'd been given was, indeed, blue—the paper on the walls, the Persian rugs on the floor, the bedspread on the large bed, and the curtains over the windows. All were in varying shades of blue, from the delicate hue of a robin's egg to the vibrant color of an indigo bunting. And when she returned to the room after her bath, instead of her own travel-stained clothes, she found a dress—every bit as lovely as the violet silk Corinne had worn earlier that day—laid out on the bed. Beside it were all the necessary undergarments. Silver picked up the dress and held it against her chest. It seemed it would be a perfect fit.

From somewhere in the house a clock chimed the quarter hour. She'd best get dressed or she would be late for supper. After the kindness of her hostess, she didn't want to appear rude. She dropped the towel and began to dress.

Beyond the bedroom door, the house came alive with sounds. Footsteps. Closing doors. Soft voices. Silver had thought Corinne Duvall lived in this big house by herself with just her servants. Obviously she'd been mistaken.

At a minute before the hour, Silver opened the bedroom door and made her way down the grand staircase and across the parquet floor, guided to the dining room by the female voices spilling into the hallway through an open door. Her stomach seemed filled with butterflies.

She stopped beneath the transom and surveyed the room.

The women were arrayed in a spectrum of colors, no two the same. There must have been close to twenty of them, ranging in age from fifteen or sixteen to perhaps thirty or so. Jewelry glittered at their throats and on their earlobes and fingers. They stood in small bunches, visiting, laughing. On the table, fine china and crystal sparkled in the light shed by the candelabras.

What on earth would Jared think of this?

She clenched her jaw, the thought unwelcome. What did she care what Jared Newman thought? He'd left her without a backward glance. Not so much as a by-your-leave.

Squaring her shoulders, she stepped into the dining room.

Chapter 27

Each girl had a story of her own, some of the stories exciting, most of them sad. As the sumptuous meal was served by Corinne's servants, Silver heard bits and pieces from each of them in turn. With every new story, Silver's understanding of this house and its inhabitants grew.

Corinne Duvall had saved all of them from a life of starvation or abuse or prostitution. In return for a place to stay, good food to eat, and fine clothes to wear, the girls worked in Corinne's Rainbow Saloon. But they were not the usual dance hall girls, serving liquor to drunken miners—or worse. They were forbidden intimacies beyond simple conversation. But, according to the girl seated on Silver's left, there was the occasional love story that ended in a wedding.

She learned one more thing during the meal. The Rainbow Saloon had honest gambling tables, and because of that, more men came there to gamble than any other saloon or gaming hall in all of Virginia City. If Matt Carlton was in this town, he would end up at the Rainbow sooner or later.

And if he's who Jared believes him to be, one of the girls at this table could be his next victim.

Even as a shudder passed through her, fresh resolve stiffened her spine. She meant to do everything she could to make certain there was no next victim. She wanted and needed the reward in order to help her father, but there were some things even more important than money.

Jared rode hard and fast toward Virginia City, leading Cinder behind him. He didn't stop until night began to fall around him. Once the horses were cared for, he made a fire and warmed some beans, eating because he knew he should, not because it mattered to him what it tasted like.

Several hours later, he lay on his bedroll, staring at the sliver of moon overhead. Sleep eluded him despite his weariness. All he could do was think of Silver and wonder if she was all right and imagine what might have happened to her. If she believed Jared had left her without a word, then she must hate him now.

He groaned and rolled onto his side. Discovering his money had been stolen and his note never delivered had been hard to swallow. It didn't help to know the employee of Wells, Fargo was now sitting in jail. Ultimately, what had happened was Jared's fault. He'd wanted to avoid a confrontation with Silver. That was the real reason he found himself lying on his bedroll too worried to sleep. That was the real reason Silver and Dean were in Virginia City without him there to protect them. It was his fault and no one else's.

God, keep her safe. Please keep her safe until I can find her. The prayer felt awkward, foreign. He'd pushed God away for years. Why should He listen to Jared now? And yet he pressed on. *Don't let me lose her. Not now that I've found her.*

The more he prayed, the easier it came. Until finally, a wall in his heart seemed to crumble and he felt himself stepping over the rubble into a place of trust.

After the early supper, all of the young women in their colorful gowns left the house in several carriages, bound for the Rainbow Saloon. Corinne remained behind with Silver.

"Well, what do you think?" Corinne asked as the two of them stood in the entry hall.

"What do I think?"

"Would you be willing to work for me?"

"Work for you?" She felt foolish, echoing the woman's words that way, but she couldn't seem to help it.

Corinne's smile was kind. "I assure you, you will be protected from harm."

Work in a saloon? It might not be the usual kind of saloon, but still . . . Her stepmother would die of shame. But what would happen to her and Dean if she refused?

"And you would be under no obligation to remain should you find you want to leave Virginia City."

Silver drew in a long, steadying breath. "Miss Corinne, before I give you my answer, I need to tell you why I came here. You asked earlier if it was because of a man. It is, but not the way you think."

An hour later, Silver opened the door to the third-floor bedroom, allowing a streak of yellow light to stream in from the hall. Dean sprawled across the bed, sound asleep. The sheet and blanket were twisted and shoved aside. The boy frowned as the light touched his face but didn't awaken. Silver moved quietly across the room. Stopping beside the bed, she brushed the hair on his forehead to one side with her fingertips. He mumbled some-thing unintelligible before rolling away from her.

Corinne had not seemed a bit surprised by Silver's story. She hadn't seemed to think it unusual for a young single woman to ride halfway across the country in the company of a bounty hunter while in pursuit of a thief and a killer. She hadn't thought it odd that Silver, when left behind by Jared, had continued on to Virginia City without him.

"You can rest your ankle for a few days," Corinne had said at the conclusion of their talk. "Then we will take you to the Rainbow and see if the work will suit."

What else could Silver do but agree to the arrangement? She and Dean would be housed and fed and safe. It was more than she had any right to expect.

With one last glance at the sleeping boy, she left the bedroom and descended the stairs to the second floor, making her way to the blue room. She was tired and ready for sleep. It had been an exhausting day, physically and emotionally.

She discovered a pretty satin nightgown awaiting her on the bed. It was amazing, really, the way clothes in her size seemed to appear out of thin air. She undressed, slipped the nightgown over her head, and got into bed, enjoying the feel of clean sheets on clean skin.

Never again would she fail to appreciate the luxury of simple things.

For a moment, she wondered about Jared. Where he was. What he was doing. But even thoughts of Jared couldn't keep her awake tonight, and she soon drifted into a dreamless slumber.

Chapter 28

Morning sunlight flooded the second-floor solarium where Silver reclined on a lounge. A fat, long-haired cat had curled up near her feet for a morning nap. The rest of the house seemed as lazy as the feline. Silver hadn't heard a single sound since following Nissa—a lithe, fair-haired girl close to Silver's age—into the sun-drenched room thirty minutes before.

As if to prove her wrong, the rattle of dishes reached her from the hallway. Chung entered moments later. He nodded to the two women, set the tray on a table, and left the solarium.

"You know," Silver said to Nissa, "I've been here for several days, and I've yet to hear Chung say a single word. He understands English well enough. Can't he speak it?"

"No one told you? Chung can't say anything. He has no tongue. Someone cut it out."

"How awful!"

"But he has no trouble communicating with Miss Corinne with grunts and gestures and smiles or frowns. I don't know how she would run this place without him."

Maria—one of the youngest of the girls who worked for Miss Corinne—entered the room before Silver could ask any more questions. "It is too quiet. I want to go shopping. Will either of you go with me?"

Where Nissa was tall and fair, Maria was petite and dark. Nissa's speech rolled with the cadence of the Swedes, while Maria's was sprinkled with words from her native Mexico. Silver liked them both a great deal.

Nissa shook her head. "I can't. I have some letters to write. Mama, she has written twice since I last answered."

"I'll join you, Maria." Silver rose from the lounge. "I could use some exercise, and I wouldn't mind seeing a little more of the town. Give me a few minutes to get ready, and I'll meet you out front."

Several hours later, her arms loaded with packages—all of them belonging to Maria—Silver stepped through the doorway of the Golden Emporium onto the boardwalk. Behind her she heard Maria's rapid chatter as she shared gossip with the proprietress of the store. Silver decided to unburden her arms before going back inside to retrieve Maria.

She turned and began walking toward the horse and buggy tied two stores away. She'd taken no more than a half dozen steps when she stopped and leaned against the building at her back, feeling as if the wind had been knocked out of her.

It was Bob. Bob Cassidy. Riding toward her on a tall sorrel. His brown hat had a broad brim, shading his eyes from view, but she could see his face clearly enough. Only it couldn't be Bob. She'd been beside Bob when he died. She'd seen him buried, prayed beside his grave. Bob was dead.

The man glanced in her direction, and she sucked in a breath as she pulled back, deeper into the shadows of the store awning.

Have I gone mad?

When the rider was directly opposite her, she was at last able to see the ways he didn't resemble Bob. This man had a squarer jaw and a broader build. His blond hair was darker. The way he sat on his horse was different too. Yet even knowing it wasn't Bob, she couldn't stop shaking. It felt as if she were seeing Death riding a horse.

"*Amiga*?"

Silver jumped at the sound of Maria's voice, and packages fell to the ground.

"Silver, what is wrong? Are you not well?"

"No. I'm fine. I was startled, that's all."

“You are as white as Miss Corinne’s cat.”

“I’m fine. Really. Let’s put these packages into the buggy and return to the house.”

Maria’s gaze seemed skeptical, but after a moment more, the girl picked up the spilled packages without another word.

Chapter 29

"If she's as pretty as you claim," the hotel clerk told Jared, "then you'll likely find her living with Miss Corinne."

After eight days of hard riding, Jared had camped last night a few miles outside of Virginia City. He'd been up at the crack of dawn, determined to find Silver without delay, anxious to know that she was okay. "Why is that? Who is Miss Corinne?"

"Corinne Duvall. She owns the Rainbow Saloon. Fanciest place this side of the Mississippi, I reckon. Some folk here in town turn their noses up at her 'cause of her past. But I kinda admire what she's done. For herself and others too. Guess no one could call Miss Corinne a real lady, but she keeps those girls from goin' down a bad road, if'n you know what I mean."

Jared wasn't sure if he understood or not, but he didn't want to waste any more time trying to find out. "Where do I find this Miss Duvall?"

"Just turn left at the bank, and you'll see the house up on the hillside. Can't miss it. Looks like a palace, it does. And she's got terraces all around with flowers growing everywhere. Don't know how her gardener gets 'em to grow like that. My missus surely can't."

Jared thanked the man and left the hotel lobby. The pinto and Cinder stood in the street, tied to a post. Jared stepped into the saddle and rode in the direction the clerk had indicated, turning at the bank. There was no doubt he'd gone in the right direction, not once the house on the hillside came into view. It did resemble a palace.

A circular drive brought him to the hitching rail in front of the veranda. He dismounted and tied the horses, then went up the steps into the shade of the porch. He removed his hat and smoothed his hair with his free hand. The air was still and already growing warm. In the distance, he heard the sounds of the mines—ore cars rolling on tracks, the grind of heavy chains, the rumble of wagons, the pounding of picks—but here on this hillside, there was an aura of serenity.

Just who was this Corinne Duvall?

He rapped on the door.

From the corner of his eye, he saw a lace curtain flutter at the window. High-pitched giggles reached him from beyond the beveled glass. He turned his head, but the curtains dropped back into place. At the same moment, the door opened. A slightly built Oriental man, clad all in black, stared up at him, saying nothing.

"I'm looking for Miss Matlock. Miss Silver Matlock. I was told she might be staying with Corinne Duvall. Is she here?"

The manservant motioned for Jared to follow

him, and he was led into a large parlor and left there. An enormous painting commanded his attention from the far end of the room. He walked toward it, captured by the look of love on the subject's face. He supposed it must be a portrait of the lady of the house. If so, she was a remarkable-looking woman. Not to mention wealthy. He'd been in some fine homes in his life, but nothing like this.

"Chung tells me you are looking for Silver."

He turned around. It was the woman in the portrait, older now but just as beautiful. She wore a morning gown of sunshine yellow, something light and breezy with plenty of froth around her neck and wrists.

"I don't believe I've seen you at the Rainbow. Are you new to Virginia City?" She indicated they should be seated.

"Yes, ma'am. Just got here this morning." He sat in the nearby chair. "I'm a friend of Miss Matlock's and was told she might be staying with you."

"Ah." She raised a brow, her expression thoughtful. "So you're the one."

"Pardon me?"

"Nothing." She smiled. "We seem to have forgotten the formalities. I'm Corinne Duvall."

"Jared Newman."

"A pleasure, Mr. Newman. Silver is here, but she isn't up yet."

Not up by this hour? That wasn't like her. "Is she ill?"

"No, she isn't ill. But it is rather early for callers. I'll let her know that you're here and see if she's ready to receive you."

There was a light rapping on Silver's door and then Corinne's voice. "Silver, may I come in?"

She groaned and rolled onto her other side, pulling the pillow over her head.

"My dear, you have a gentleman caller."

A gentleman caller? She'd been working at the Rainbow Saloon for only a week, but she knew Corinne Duvall's rules. She didn't allow men to call on her girls at the house. Not unless there was a serious relationship developing that might lead to marriage.

Corinne entered the room and came to the side of the bed. She gently pulled away the pillow. "Are you unwell? I can tell Mr. Newman you're not able to receive him."

"Mr. Newman?" Fully awake in an instant, Silver sat up. "Jared's here?"

"Yes. In the parlor. He seems quite anxious to see you." Corinne smiled. "He is your bounty hunter. Yes?"

Jared was here. She'd thought he'd left for good, but he was here and asking for her. Her heart raced at the news. It shouldn't make her feel so relieved. She should stay angry with him.

He'd left her, after all. But now he was here, and that was all that seemed to matter to her.

"Shall I tell Mr. Newman you will see him, or shall I send him away?"

"I'll see him." She pushed aside the bedding. "I'll be down shortly."

Corinne chuckled as she turned away. "I'll tell him."

As soon as the other woman left the room, Silver rose and hurriedly washed and dressed, her mind churning the entire time. What would she say to him? What would he say to her? Should she forgive him at once for abandoning her and Dean in Winnemucca? Or should she make him suffer first?

Jared felt himself being observed from the doorway.

He turned and met the curious gazes of two girls. They were young, midteens at most, both of them wearing morning gowns similar to the one Corinne Duvall had worn, except the colors were different. Were these her daughters? He doubted it. They looked nothing like her. One was a redhead, the other a brunette.

"Hello," he said.

They giggled.

Ah. They were the ones who had watched him through the window. He stood. "I've come to see Miss Matlock. Do you live here too?"

The redhead opened her mouth to reply but was cut short by Corinne's reappearance.

"Idonna. Helene."

They jumped and turned toward the woman.

"Can you explain what you're doing here?"

"No, Miss Corinne," they answered in unison.

"Then I believe you had best excuse yourselves and return to your room. We'll talk about this later."

They obeyed without a backward glance.

"They weren't bothering me," Jared said.

"Perhaps not, Mr. Newman," Corinne replied as she came toward him. "But they know the rules."

"Rules?"

"Gentlemen callers are rarely received. Only on very special occasions. As for those two?" Her smile was tender. "Idonna and Helene are much too young to entertain gentlemen callers at any time."

"Where is Silver?"

"She'll be down presently. In the meantime, let's sit down. Oh, good. The coffee is here." She settled onto a sofa. "Chung is the most remarkable man. I have two maids who help with the housework and a wonderful woman to do the cooking. And, of course, there's the groom to care for the horses. But Chung truly runs every-thing. Did you see the gardens? They are his creation."

"Very pretty," he replied, not caring one bit about her gardens.

Corinne poured coffee into a china cup and held it out to him. He took it, then set it on a table next to his chair. He wanted answers, but he wasn't going to get them from this woman. He could tell that.

"Hello, Jared."

His pulse jumped at the sound of Silver's voice. He rose and turned toward the doorway.

He hardly recognized her. The simple blouse and split riding skirt were gone. In their place she wore a rose-colored gown that had to be in the latest style. It made her look like royalty, framed by the archway, holding her slender form erect, her head high, her expression sure and proud. Trail dust was gone, as was the exhaustion that had weighed upon her shoulders for the weeks they were together. A beautiful, confident woman had replaced the desperate girl.

"I didn't know if I would ever see you again." She moved toward him, accompanied by the soft swish of silk skirts.

"I can explain."

"Can you? I believe I'd like to hear that." She turned toward Corinne Duvall. "May we have some privacy, Miss Corinne?"

"You know the rules," the woman answered, "but I shall withdraw across the parlor."

Jared longed to put her from the room, forcibly

if necessary. Instead he drew Silver to the mantel beneath Corinne's portrait. "What is this place? Where's Dean? Are you all right?"

"Dean is here. We're both fine." Her voice was soft and calm, but he heard the hurt all the same.

"I didn't just leave you in Winnemucca."

Silver's eyebrows rose.

"No, I did leave you, but there was a good reason. I heard Carlton might be in jail up in Idaho Territory, so I went to see if it was him."

"And it wasn't," she said.

"No, it wasn't."

"So you came to Virginia City to find him."

"No, I came to find you."

The look she gave him said she didn't believe him yet.

He pressed on. "Before I caught the stage to Silver City, I sent you a note of explanation along with money to hold you over until I got back. I was wrong not to tell you in person. And I sure never expected the clerk would keep the money himself. I couldn't believe it when I got back and found you'd sold Cinder and caught the train to come here on your own."

"What else could I do?" she asked softly. "I had only a little money, and you were gone."

You could have waited for me. You should have trusted me. "I brought Cinder with me."

"Cinder?" Silver whispered, eyes widening again.

He jerked his head in the general direction of the front door. “She’s tied up outside.”

“You bought her back from the blacksmith?”

“Yes.”

“How could you afford it?”

“Wells, Fargo didn’t want a disgruntled customer saying their agents can’t be trusted. They gave me back what was stolen and then some. Enough to take us back to Colorado if we’re careful.”

“Back to Colorado,” Silver said softly, then walked back to the settee and sat, folding her hands in her lap.

He followed and sat beside her.

She stared at her hands. “A week ago I saw a man who looked like Bob. It frightened me, even though I knew it couldn’t be him. It made me wonder if I should ever have hired you to chase Bob down. I’ve become so obsessed with getting the money and jewels back or maybe getting some of the reward for Matt Carlton, and it’s made me imagine things and make foolish choices.”

Jared had thought her foolish too, but he understood a thing or two about that kind of obsession.

“If Miss Corinne hadn’t rescued Dean and me off the streets of Virginia City, I don’t know what would have become of us.”

“I’m here now,” he said. “I’ll take care of you.”

"Why?" She looked up. "Why would you?"

Because I've fallen in love with you.

"Why, Jared?"

"I hoped you'd know why."

He placed the flat of his hand against her cheek. All he wanted to do was draw her into his arms and kiss her until they were both breathless. He wanted to take her in his arms and carry her out of this house and out of this town. He wanted to put an end to the old chapter of his life. He wanted something better, something finer, some-thing new. He wanted Silver.

Corinne Duvall cleared her throat, and Jared stopped himself from following his instincts. A good thing too. He needed to capture Matt Carlton. He couldn't have something better and finer and new without putting an end to the old, once and for all.

He rose to his feet. "I'm going to talk to the sheriff and look around Virginia City. But I promise you this, Silver: I won't leave again without you. Not for any reason. I think you're safe here with this woman, or I'd take you and the boy with me right now. I'll be back for you. Trust me."

Chapter 30

The man from the street, the one who looked so much like Bob Cassidy, was in the Rainbow Saloon that night, playing poker. And when Silver saw him from across the vast public room, her reaction was the same as it had been before. Surprise. Shock. Dread.

But it's not Bob. It's not him, no matter how much he looks like him. Bob is dead. Jared buried him.

Jared. She would concentrate her thoughts on Jared instead of that stranger. She had no reason to be afraid of anything now. Jared had promised he would return for her. She would watch for him. She would watch for him tonight and, if needed, the next night and the next. She would watch for him here at the Rainbow in the evenings, and she would watch for him on the road leading to the Duvall home in the daytime.

"I hoped you'd know why." The memory of his words and the way he'd said them poured over her like warm honey. It might be crazy, but she did know why. Why he'd bought back her horse. Why he'd come to Virginia City. Now. At last. Somewhere between Twin Springs and Virginia City, she'd learned to love him—and he'd learned to love her too.

It worked . . . a little. Thinking about Jared made her forget for a time the man who resembled Bob. Made her forget him right up until he left the card table and came across the vast room to where she stood, momentarily alone.

"Pardon me. Is your name Silver, by any chance? Silver Matlock?"

Her stomach seemed to drop and her breath catch. How could he know her name? He was a stranger to her.

"I see I have surprised you."

She looked around for one of several men Corinne employed to protect her girls and keep order in the saloon. They all seemed to have disappeared.

"Might we sit down and talk for a bit?" The man motioned toward an unoccupied corner.

She didn't want to go with him, didn't want to be near someone who reminded her of her erstwhile fiancé, now dead and buried on a homestead in eastern Nevada. But providing feminine conversation and company was what Corinne had hired her to do. What else could she do but nod and walk to the indicated settee?

The stranger sat beside her, a polite distance away. "When I saw you, I couldn't believe it was really you. You are even more beautiful than your photograph."

Her pulse hiccupped again. "My photograph?"

"The one my brother carried with him."

"Your brother?"

"Robert. Robert Cassidy."

Bob's brother? She'd thought him dead too. Hadn't Bob told her his half brother was dead?

"My half brother," he said, confirming her thoughts. "We got our looks from our mother rather than our different fathers." He smiled slowly. "My name is Carlton. Matthew Carlton."

Her blood turned to ice in her veins. This man had murdered time and again. And now he knew who she was.

"I'm curious to know how you wound up in Virginia City, Miss Matlock."

She forced a soft laugh, pretending an ease she didn't feel. "I'm not sure how it happened myself."

"Please. Amuse me." His gaze was as sharp as a razor.

Think, Silver. You must think clearly. "When did Bob show you my photograph?" she asked.

"We came to Nevada together."

Silver had admired the actors and actresses she'd seen in the theater in Denver. She hoped she could be a good actress herself and play a convincing part. "Is Bob here in Virginia City with you? Is he here in this saloon?" She let her gaze sweep the room, as if looking for the man she knew was dead.

"No. Bob isn't here."

She looked at Carlton again. "You must know,

of course, that he left me at the church on our wedding day."

"Yes. I knew. I'm sorry he hurt you." He was the better actor. His words sounded genuine.

"I'm surprised he kept the photograph I gave him."

"My brother never had much backbone. Perhaps you were too much woman for him." His smile returned, broader this time. "I would not have left you behind."

His words made her skin crawl. What a fool she was, to have thought she could chase down this ruthless killer on her own. It took all of her resolve not to rise and run away from him.

"Please continue with your story, Miss Matlock. Tell me why you are here and not back in Colorado with your parents."

Silver stiffened her spine and lifted her chin. "Before he left Twin Springs, Bob broke into my father's safe and took everything of value. He ruined us. The bank will take my father's store and our home. I don't know where my parents will go when that happens." Enough of the truth. Now back to the performance. "I couldn't be a burden on my father and stepmother. Not when I was the reason for their ruin. So I came west to forge a new life for myself. Someone I met on the train mentioned Virginia City and Miss Duvall's Rainbow Saloon. It sounded . . . safe. So here I am."

"So here you are," he echoed softly.

• • •

Jared had been inside a dozen saloons already, looking for Matt Carlton. But he hadn't come to the Rainbow to find Carlton. He'd come to the Rainbow because he wanted to see Silver again before he bedded down for the night somewhere beyond the borders of the town.

When he saw Silver on that settee, his first response was jealousy. He didn't want her sitting and talking to any other man. He wanted her to himself. But then the man turned his head, and Jared got a good look at his face. He looked a lot like Bob Cassidy. He looked—

And then the puzzle pieces fell into place in his mind. It seemed so obvious. That man was Matt Carlton, and he resembled Cassidy because they were related. But at the moment, what Jared cared about most was the woman seated with Carlton. Had she any idea of the danger she could be in, bringing herself to Carlton's attention?

He forced himself to study every detail of Carlton's appearance, from the color of his hair to the patrician lines of his face to the fancy suit he wore. He looked every inch the refined gentleman, moneyed and educated. But Matt Carlton was no gentleman. He was an animal, and if he took an interest in Silver—

That thought spurred Jared forward. His advantage was knowing who Carlton was and Carlton not knowing the same in return. Did he even know a bounty hunter had been looking for his trail for six years? Maybe. Maybe not.

Silver glanced up as he drew near. Relief flashed in her eyes. “Good evening, Mr. Newman.”

“Miss Matlock.” He gave her a nod. “A pleasure to see you again.”

She smiled briefly.

“I apologize for interrupting.” Jared looked at Carlton, then back to Silver. “But I do need to speak with you for a moment, Miss Matlock. It’s important.”

With a nod, she excused herself and rose from the settee. Jared offered his arm, ignoring the irritated look Matt Carlton shot his way. She took Jared’s arm.

“Do you know who that was?” Jared demanded in a low voice as soon as they were out of hearing distance.

“Bob Cassidy’s half brother.”

Jared stopped. “Does he know who you are?”

Silver nodded.

This wasn’t good. Not good at all. Matt Carlton had been able to avoid the authorities for years because he’d left no clues. Little physical description other than that scar. No name to go on either. He wasn’t a fool. He would wonder why his brother’s jilted bride was in the same city he was in. It would make him suspicious. As it should.

“I’ll need to act fast,” Jared said, thoughts

churning. "Before he has a chance to leave town."

"He might not leave. I told him I came because Bob's theft ruined my parents financially. I think he believed me. So why should he go anywhere else?"

Jared had to fight the urge to look behind him. He didn't like not knowing where Carlton was, but he didn't want to appear interested in the man either. "He's nobody's fool. He suspects some-thing. I guarantee it. I can't do anything in a place like this. He's not a wanted man in Nevada. I got the feeling when I talked to the sheriff that he wasn't interested in the story I had to tell. I'll need to get Carlton away from town where there isn't a crowd before I take him into custody. We've got to get him back to Colorado where that girl in Central City can identify him by his scar. It won't do us a bit of good if he is sitting in a jail cell here. And besides, the sheriff would need more evidence than our say-so. He'd be free in no time."

"I could get him away from the Rainbow. Someplace you could apprehend him."

He frowned.

"I could ask him to meet me somewhere so we could talk privately."

"No." Jared shook his head. "That's too risky."

She gave him one of her determined looks. "It's why I'm here. It's why we're both here. And what danger could I be in if you're nearby?"

"Silver—"

"I'm going to help you whether you like it or not."

He didn't doubt it for an instant. "All right, Silver. We'll come up with a plan together. The two of us."

Chapter 31

Early the next morning, Silver went to talk to Corinne. In her brief time in the Duvall home, she'd come to feel a great affection for everyone who lived within its brick walls, especially for the mistress of the house.

"Come in," Corinne called when Silver knocked on the door to her bedroom suite.

"I hope I'm not disturbing you."

"Not at all." Corinne lay on a lounge chair, holding a china cup in one hand.

"I . . . I've come to tell you I'm leaving Virginia City."

"With Mr. Newman?"

"Yes."

"I thought you would the first time I met him."

Silver cleared her throat as she settled on a nearby chair. "He is here, Miss Corinne."

"Mr. Newman is here?" She looked toward the door, as if expecting to find Jared standing there.

"No. Not Jared. The man we followed from

Colorado. He is here in Virginia City. He was at the Rainbow last night. I . . . I spoke with him."

Corinne straightened. "The man who killed Dean's parents?"

Silver nodded.

"Are you in danger? Does he know you followed him?"

"I don't think so."

Corinne leaned back again. "Well, thank goodness for that."

"I have a favor to ask, Miss Corinne."

The woman cocked an eyebrow in question.

"I told you before how Dean came to be with me. With us."

"Yes?"

"May I leave him here until . . . until this is over? I don't want to put him in danger. But I'll come back for him as soon as it's safe."

Concern flooded Corinne's face. "Will *you* be safe, my dear?"

She thought of Jared. He was strong. He was smart. He was determined. She trusted him. She loved him. She wouldn't doubt him again.

"Yes," she answered confidently. "I'll be safe."

A short while later, her conversation with Corinne Duvall completed, Silver went looking for Dean. She finally spied him kneeling on the flat stones that surrounded the pond and fountain at the center of the terraced gardens. He leaned forward at the waist, staring intently into the water.

"Dean?" Silver called as she drew near. "Don't fall in."

He didn't look up. "I won't."

"What are you doing?"

"Just watchin' the goldfish."

Silver couldn't help noting the changes the past week of good food and plenty of sleep and the kindness of the women in the house had wrought in Dean. He was so much more the little boy he was meant to be. She wasn't foolish enough to believe the pain and anger of losing his parents were so swiftly forgotten. But for today, for this moment, he was merely a child at play. She wanted to make certain he could continue that way in the future.

"Come over here, please." She settled onto a nearby bench and patted the space beside her.

Dean dropped a couple of small pebbles into the pond. Then he jumped to his feet and came to her. "Is Mr. Newman comin' back today? You said he might."

"Perhaps." Silver put her arm around his shoulders. "Dean, I have something important to ask you. When . . . when I leave Virginia City, I want you to go with me. To Colorado. Would you like to do that?"

He tipped his head, peering up at her with a puzzled expression. "I thought that's what I was doing all along. I mean, you coulda left me plenty of times if you'd wanted. You coulda left me with that sheriff."

"Yes." She offered a fleeting smile. "That's true."

"Will Mr. Newman be goin' to Colorado too?"

The plan she had concocted with Jared the previous night flitted through her mind. If all went well today, the three of them *and* Matt Carlton would be going to Colorado. But she couldn't tell Dean that. She wanted him to continue to drop pebbles into a pond and watch fat goldfish swim about in the murky depths for as long as possible.

"Yes," she answered at last.

"Then I reckon it's a good idea."

"I'm glad." She gave his shoulders a squeeze.

"Miss Silver?"

"Mmm."

"What am I gonna ride when we go? Mr. Newman sold the packhorse."

"Don't you worry, Dean. We'll figure that out when the time comes." *And if all goes well today, that time is almost here*. She rose from the bench. "I have an errand to do in town, but I'll see you before . . . before bedtime. Mind Miss Corinne."

"Sure." The boy hopped up and hurried back to the edge of the pond. "See ya later."

Jared, his hat brim pulled low on his forehead, stepped into the spacious lobby of the Grant

Hotel. His eyes swept the room. There was a gentleman seated near the window, a folded newspaper in one hand, a smoking pipe in the other. Another man, accompanied by his wife, stood before the desk. The clerk stared down his nose as he observed the guest signing in. A bellboy waited off to one side, his arms laden with luggage. Through an arched doorway, Jared saw tables covered with white linen cloths. Waitresses in crisp aprons and caps bustled about, serving breakfast.

Jared had told Silver he would watch for her arrival in the restaurant of the Grant. He selected a table with a clear view of the lobby and sat with his back to the wall. When the waitress came, he ordered coffee. Then he settled in to wait—and even said a quick prayer that all would go accord-ing to plan. After a long silence, he was finding it easier these days to talk with God. Something he had Silver to thank for.

Silver arrived at the agreed-upon time, looking beautiful in one of the dresses Corinne Duvall had provided. Soon enough, she would change into the clothes she'd worn on her way to Nevada. He would be glad to see her in riding skirt and blouse. It was the way she'd looked when he learned to love her.

Jared knew she saw him, even though she didn't look his way.

He watched as she turned toward the staircase

and smiled. Which meant Matt Carlton was coming down to meet her. Her note must have worked. All Jared could do now was hope he didn't come to regret giving in to this plan of hers.

Carlton stepped into view, and Jared tensed. He was so close. So close to bringing in the man who'd murdered his family. So close to putting an end to this chapter of his life. So close to starting over, becoming something better.

Be careful, Silver. Whatever you do, be careful!

Nerves erupted with fresh fury in Silver's stomach as Matt Carlton stopped the horse and buggy in a meadow surrounded by scrub pine and firs. They were a good distance from town and the mines. The only sounds were the buzz of insects and the whisper of a hot breeze through the dry grass.

Carlton pulled some blankets from the back of Corinne's buggy, along with the picnic basket Silver had brought with her, and placed them in the shade. Then he returned and offered his hand to help her down. She had to force herself to take it. Only knowing Jared watched from somewhere nearby let her do it.

Matt Carlton, she realized, had soulless eyes, and it made her want to shudder. She subdued the reaction.

"I confess to great curiosity, Miss Matlock,"

he said as he escorted her to the shade. “Why did you send that note? Why did you want this assignation?”

“I would hardly call it that, Mr. Carlton. I merely want to know why Bob left the way he did. On our wedding day. I want to understand why he stole from my father. I . . . I need to understand, and I didn’t want to talk about private matters where we would risk being overheard.” She sank onto the blanket. “Besides, you were almost my brother-in-law, and I’m so very far from my family.” She ended with a shrug.

“I see.” He sat nearby.

Too near for her comfort. It took all her will not to move away from him.

A slow smile curved his lips. “My brother left Twin Springs and you because I told him to.”

“Why would you do such a thing? You didn’t know me. You didn’t know anything about me. You’d never even seen my photograph until after he left Twin Springs. You said so last night.”

“No, but I wish now that I had seen you first.”

Soulless, soulless eyes. Again she had to contain the urge to shiver with dread.

A movement caught her eye beyond Matt Carlton’s shoulder. Jared, stepping from behind a tree. He shook his head, silently warning her not to give him away. Afraid she might do so, she lowered her eyes to her hands, folded in her lap.

"Where is Bob now?" she asked softly, as if she didn't already know the answer.

"He's dead."

There was a soft sound of a hammer being cocked, then Jared said, "Don't move, Carlton. Not an inch."

Silver scrambled to her feet and away from Matt Carlton. She rubbed her arms as if trying to scrub away his proximity.

"What do you want?" Carlton asked. "If it's money, I'll see that you get it."

Jared ignored him. "Stand up and put your hands behind your back."

"Who are you?"

"The name's Newman. And what I want is to see you hang."

"Hang. What for?" Carlton got to his feet and put his hands behind him as ordered.

Carlton sounded calm and unconcerned. It made Silver nervous. Was there a flaw in their plan? Could he get away?

"For murder." Jared snapped handcuffs onto his prisoner's wrists. Then he searched him, removing the key to his hotel room from one pocket along with a small pistol from a strap under his arm.

"You aren't the law," the prisoner continued to protest.

"No. I'm not."

"You have no authority to take me in. What

evidence do you have that I'm guilty of murder?"

Jared took the collar of Carlton's shirt in his left hand and yanked. Buttons popped and fabric tore. "That scar." He touched Carlton's collarbone. "That scar's my evidence."

"It won't be enough to hold me, and you know it. Who says they saw it? There isn't anyone alive who's seen it. As soon as we get back to town, the sheriff will have to turn me loose. You know that."

"True enough. Which is why you aren't going back to Virginia City."

Carlton turned his head and looked at Silver. Eyes that had been cold and empty were now filled with hatred. "You're a part of this, aren't you?"

"Did you shoot Bob?" she asked, ignoring his question. "Did you kill your own brother like you killed that man and his wife?"

He made a sound that was part laughter, part growl.

"Come on." Jared grabbed Carlton by the upper arm and pulled him to the nearest tree where he tied him up. Then he walked over to Silver. "Are you all right?" His voice was low, the look in his eyes gentle.

She nodded.

"You sure you'll be all right while I'm gone?" He withdrew one of his revolvers and gave it to her. "Don't get close to him. Keep that pointed at him and use it if he makes a wrong move."

She nodded again.

"I'll search his room. If there's money or jewels left, I'll find them. I'll return with the horses and Dean as fast as I can."

Strange how her nerves quieted, how the fear vanished. It didn't matter that Jared had yet to say he loved her; she knew that he did. And that was enough of a promise for now.

"I'll be fine, Jared. Just hurry."

Chapter 32

The next morning, Silver opened her eyes to find a cloudy, pewter-colored sky. Dawn had yet to arrive. She sat up, pursing her lips as she arched her back to relieve a crimp in her spine. It amazed her how much harder the ground felt now than before she'd spent those nights in the blue room of Miss Corinne's house. She missed that comfort-able bed more than she cared to admit.

She glanced to her left. Dean's face was hidden beneath his blanket, only the top of his head showing. Had she been wrong to bring him with them? Selfish, even? The trip before them was arduous and long. Was she putting a young boy in unnecessary danger because she'd grown so fond of him and couldn't let go?

She glanced to her right. Jared's bedroll was empty. She wasn't surprised. He would want them to make an early start. They'd put a good distance between them and Virginia City yesterday, but he would want many miles every day. He wanted them back to Denver as fast as the horses could get them there. If only Jared had found any of her father's stolen property in Matt Carlton's room. But he hadn't. It was all gone.

Silver refrained from looking at the prisoner, who was secured to a tree a good distance beyond where Jared had slept. She tried not to dwell too much upon the fate of her parents if there wasn't a reward to collect. She needed to cling to the hope that there would be.

Jared appeared over the top of a rise and descended the incline, his arms laden with firewood. He glanced at the prisoner first, then at Silver, and finally dropped the wood and began to rekindle the campfire.

"Where are you taking me, Newman?" Carlton demanded, breaking the silence of the morning.

Silver liked it better when he kept his mouth shut.

Jared answered, "We're taking you to Denver. And then maybe on to Central City."

Silver took satisfaction in the surprise that flashed across Matt Carlton's face. He'd been so smug before, so sure of himself. Even Jared's knowledge of the scar hadn't shaken him. But the name of the town in Colorado did. Good. It should worry him.

"You've got the wrong man," the prisoner blustered. "I'm not who you think I am."

"I haven't got the wrong man, and we both know it. You remember Felicity. You worked in the same saloon with her. She didn't die, Carlton, like you thought she would. She's waiting to testify against you. You hid your face well, but she remembers that scar. And she remembers everything you said to her." Jared left the fire and walked toward Carlton. "My sister didn't live long, but she lived long enough to describe that scar and to let me know what you did to her. And you're going to swing for it." His right hand dropped to the revolver in his holster.

An alarm sounded in Silver's head. "Jared?"

He didn't turn around.

Louder this time, "Jared."

This time, he heard her. His hand moved away from the gun as he faced her.

She shook her head and tried to tell him with her eyes that hate and revenge wouldn't serve their purpose. All they had to do was make it to Denver with their prisoner. Then they could forget Matt Carlton and never think of him again.

The need for revenge had burned hot inside Jared for many years. In the past, those feelings hadn't disturbed him. He'd nurtured them, even. Hate had kept him going when he was tired or hungry or discouraged, when he remembered his parents and sister, when he thought about the other victims Matt Carlton had left behind. But something was different now. He was different now. Silver had changed him. She'd made him want a different life, made him believe he could have something better. *Be* something better.

As he'd done all the way to Nevada, Jared pushed the horses and their riders hard. The small party stopped around noon for a quick meal before moving on. The overcast sky grew darker as the day lengthened. He hoped the rain would hold off. The journey was hard enough without being wet through.

As their first full day on the trail neared its end, Jared's thoughts began to darken like the skies overhead. Doubt replaced hope. Who was he kidding, thinking he might make a life with Silver? Even with a reward for Carlton's capture, he wouldn't have anything to offer her. Her parents wouldn't want her to marry a man like him. He'd thought at one time that finding Carlton would allow him to go home again, but he knew better. Fair Acres belonged to someone else. The gentleman's son he'd once been was gone too. Forever gone.

He hadn't told Silver he loved her. She'd never said she loved him. Sometimes her eyes seemed to say it, but maybe that was his own wishful thinking. She'd joined him in this venture because she was desperate to save her family from ruin. She'd joined him because she believed herself to be the cause of those troubles. But once they returned to Colorado, once she was surrounded by family and friends, she would forget the bounty hunter. As she should.

With luck, they'd be in Denver in four weeks. Just four more weeks. That was all the time he had left with Silver.

Chapter 33

After five days on the trail, it all felt familiar to Silver again. Rise early. Eat something unappetizing. Break camp. Ride hard. Make camp. Eat something unappetizing. Tend the horses. Fall into their bedrolls exhausted. Everyone seemed too tired to talk, and the days were filled with silence once again. Sometimes the routine seemed like the only life she'd ever known.

The first quarter moon hung suspended above the eastern horizon as Silver sat on her bedroll. The campfire over which they had prepared their supper had burned low, hot coals turning from red to white. Jared stood just beyond the pale glow of the fire with his back toward her, his stance nonchalant, yet she sensed an underlying current of tension. He was always on alert, always looking for danger. She might have asked what troubled him, but he'd erected an invisible barrier, keeping her at arm's length.

How she wished she could go to him, put her arms around him, help shoulder the burden. How she wished she could tell him all that was in her heart.

Loving Jared Newman, she had realized, was the single most important thing she'd done. And she hadn't done it to please anyone else. She'd spent years trying to conform herself to be what her stepmother expected. Or, failing that, doing her best to be the opposite of what was wanted. But she loved Jared because of the good man he was, the man she could see even when he couldn't see it himself.

A sound came from behind her. It was Dean, thrashing in his sleep. Another nightmare. He'd started having them the first night on the trail. Traveling so close to the killer of his parents had driven away the fragile peace he'd found at Miss Corinne's house.

She reached out, placed a hand on the boy's back, and murmured some comforting words. A short while later, he quieted, but Silver didn't move away. She remained, still touching him, as she prayed for all of them—Jared and Dean and herself—that they would find a stronger and lasting peace in their hearts when they reached Denver and were rid of their prisoner.

Jared watched Silver as she comforted the restless boy. She was a natural with children, whether she knew it or not. A firm but kind voice. A gentle touch. She would make some lucky kid a good mother.

As if sensing his observance, she turned her head, found him with her eyes, and smiled. Then she rose and came toward him. "I think he'll sleep peacefully now."

"We probably should have left him with Corinne Duvall."

"I've wondered the same. But I couldn't do it. He's . . . he's like family to me now." She placed her fingers on his forearm. "Besides, he needs to see justice done. You must understand that better than anyone."

"He didn't see Carlton when his parents died. He can't testify against him."

"No, but he remembers the aftermath. He—" Her voice caught and tears welled.

Jared couldn't help himself. He drew her close, wrapping his arms around her, loving the feel of her cheek against his chest. It didn't matter that there were dozens of reasons why he wasn't good enough for Silver. It didn't matter that he had nothing of value to offer her. Right now, what she needed most was comfort—and that much he could do for her. “You need to get some sleep,” he said softly near her ear.

She drew her head back and looked up at him. “I don’t need sleep as much as I need you to hold me.”

Satisfaction that she’d actually voiced her feelings warred with his reticence to act on them. He sighed. “I’m no good for you, Silver. You know that.”

“You’re wrong about that. You’re so very, very wrong.”

“I’m not much better than he is.” Jared jerked his head toward Matt Carlton, asleep by the tree to which he was chained. “I’ve wanted to kill him with my bare hands. I’ve wanted to watch him die, slowly and painfully.” He released her and took a step back.

“But don’t you see? That’s what makes you different from him and others like him. No matter how badly you want to dole out punishment, no matter how much you desire revenge, you don’t take it. You didn’t kill Carlton and pretend it was justice.”

“I’ve killed other men.”

“Men who were shooting at you first. You saved the life of the sheriff back in Green River. Remember?”

“Silver, it isn’t—”

“I’ve seen the man you really are, Jared.” She framed his face with the palms of her hands.

"You are good and tender and caring. With me. With Dean." She moved one hand down to press flat against his chest. "I've seen the love you've hidden in your heart. I'll wait until you see it too."

Even if all she said was true, even if he was the man she thought him to be, it didn't change what he'd done or how he'd lived these past six years. It didn't change that he still had nothing to offer her.

"Don't wait, Silver. You'll be wasting your time."

Before he could forget himself and kiss her, he turned and walked into the darkness.

Chapter 34

The strain began to tell on all of them. Some days they covered forty miles, resting only for the sake of the horses. They stayed away from towns and the rail line. Their food consisted of whatever fresh game Jared happened to find, supplemented with hardtack and beans, and even those supplies were running low. The temperatures soared into the nineties and higher, sweltering heat during the day that chilled quickly after the sun went down.

The journey would have been hard enough on its own without the added unpleasantness of Matt Carlton's presence. For Silver, it was especially trying. She didn't like the way he watched her. His eyes were full of evil, and at times it seemed that evil reached out to touch her, like tentacles of a sea monster.

Dean cut Carlton a wide berth, but his eyes were full of hate. Silver tried talking to the boy about it, tried to show him that hatred never made things better. But he was only a child. Could he understand? She didn't know.

Silver began praying for Dean every night, asking God to cut the anger from his heart. She asked God to do the same for Jared. She asked Him to heal the old wounds and make him new. And she prayed that God would keep all of them safe and bring them into a new and brighter place.

It was late in the afternoon of their tenth day on the trail when Carlton's mount pulled up lame.

"It's a bad bruise." Jared lowered the animal's leg. "We'll have to take it easy on him for a few days." He glanced around. "We'll make camp here."

Silver breathed a sigh. Their campsite was in a mountain pass with trees and a nearby stream instead of the interminable desert and sage. She knew more desert lay beyond this respite, but she meant to enjoy this spot—and the early stop—while she could.

Jared shot a couple of quail, and Silver roasted the birds over the fire. After they'd eaten supper, she slipped away to bathe for the first time in what seemed ages.

After stripping down to her drawers and chemise, she stepped into the stream. The icy water elicited a shriek of surprise. She hadn't expected it to be so cold. She forced herself to lie flat on the smooth rocks that lined the bottom so the water almost covered her. But she couldn't stand the frigid temperature for long. She hurried to scrub herself clean, even soaping her hair twice. Then she washed her clothes before placing them across some large rocks to dry. With any luck, there was enough heat left in the day to do the job. She rubbed her damp, goose-pimpled skin with a blanket, then donned her lone change of clothes, after which she sat on a boulder and brushed her hair.

"Silver." Jared's voice came from a short distance away.

She looked behind her but couldn't see him. "I'm dressed. You can come on."

"It'll be dark soon." He stepped into view.

"I'm nearly finished." She looked away from him. "The water's like ice, but it feels good to be clean again."

Jared sat on another boulder. "We'll have to go slow tomorrow, give the horses more rest. It'll add several days to our journey, but it would be worse if we lost one of the horses altogether."

"I don't suppose it makes much difference

how long it takes." There. She'd spoken the truth aloud. "Not for my parents anyway. If there is a reward, I doubt it would be paid in time to help them. The banker gave them ninety days. It's been nearly sixty. By the time we're back . . ." She let her words drift into silence as she resumed brushing her hair.

"If there was a warrant with his name on it for his arrest, it might have been different. We could have left him in Nevada. But as it is—" He shrugged. "I'll send a telegram to Mr. Harrison as soon as I can."

She loved him for trying to offer some hope. Only one of many reasons she loved him, though she continued to keep those words to herself. For now.

If Jared kissed her, he would get lost in her.

His future was uncertain. His past was unpleasant. She thought herself in love with him. He'd seen it in her eyes, time and again. He hadn't discouraged her the way he should have. And that wasn't fair to her, and it wasn't fair to himself.

"I'd better get back to the prisoner." He pushed up from the boulder. "Don't stay out here much longer. It'll be dark soon."

He followed the trail through the trees to their campsite, stopping when it came into view. The horses, wearing hobbles, stood dozing, their tails swishing in a sleepy rhythm. The fire cast a circle of light into the gathering dusk. Carlton sat on the ground near a sturdy tree. Dean sat on a log opposite him, whittling a piece of wood. The calmness of the scene belied the nature of their journey.

How much longer would it take them to reach Denver now that one horse was lame? Silver said it no longer mattered how quickly they reached her home. It would be too late to make a difference for her parents. She might be right too. Collecting the reward Owen Harrison had offered several years back could be a long time coming, if it came at all, and so much could still go wrong.

He'd failed her, as he should have known he would. The right man, the man she deserved, wouldn't have failed her.

Chapter 35

They traveled slowly, but the injured horse didn't improve.

"You don't have any other choice, Jared," Silver told him late on the second day when they'd stopped for another rest. "We can't continue with that horse. It will have to be replaced."

It was hot—too hot to be hungry, too hot to think clearly. Sweat trickled down her back. Her muscles ached. The icy mountain stream where she'd bathed two nights before was a distant memory.

"There has to be a better way than me leaving you and Dean alone with him." Jared jerked his head toward Matt Carlton.

The prisoner had been secured, as usual, with a strong, narrow chain that went through the cuffs on the prisoner's wrists and then wrapped around a tree. It was closed with a padlock. The setup allowed Carlton some freedom of movement and a modicum of privacy when necessary but no way of escape.

"There isn't," Silver replied.

"I don't like it."

"Like it or not, it's the best option. Unless we want to sit here for a couple of weeks. Otherwise we have to have another horse, and you are the one who has to get it for us."

She could tell he wanted to protest further. She could also tell the moment when he knew she was right. There was no other way. They had to keep Carlton out of sight until they reached Colorado. That meant Jared would have to go alone to the nearest farm or ranch or town and make a trade for the horse that was lame. Silver couldn't do it. Even she realized she was safer here than riding alone on the trail. At least here she knew who the enemy was—and he was chained to a tree.

"All right, Silver. But you and Dean keep your

distance from him." Again he motioned with his head toward Carlton. "Don't remove those handcuffs. Not for any reason. No matter what he says to you. Do you understand me? Not even if a forest fire blazes through here and burns him to a crisp."

"I won't remove the handcuffs. I promise. We'll be fine."

"You've got plenty of water and enough food to see you through until I'm back. By nightfall, if all goes well."

"We'll be fine," she repeated.

Jared's eyes studied her. So long that she wondered if he might say something more. Something personal. But he didn't. At last he turned and swung onto the pinto. "Keep the revolver handy." He turned his horse away, leading the bay behind him.

Silver watched until he'd disappeared from sight—and missed him almost at once. A hot breeze whispered in the treetops. Normally she liked the sound, but not today. Today it sounded lonely, and she felt isolated from the rest of the world.

"He'll be lucky if he's able to make a trade today," Carlton said. "He might not even be back until tomorrow."

"He'll be back." She stiffened her spine. "Jared said he would be back today, and he will be. He's a man of his word." She turned toward the prisoner. “I’ll get us some hardtack to eat.”

“Where’s the boy?”

“Trying to catch a fish or two.”

“So it’s just you and me for now.”

“Be quiet.” She opened the flap on the saddlebag and peered inside.

“Afraid of me, aren’t you, Miss Matlock? You should be. I’m not weak the way my brother was. Bob was an idiot. Wouldn’t have taken him along with me to Virginia City, except I needed some traveling money, and he had a way to get it.”

Silver looked at him again, another realization dawning. “You’re the reason Bob robbed my father. He did it for you. Because you told him to do it. You coerced him, didn’t you?”

Carlton shrugged. “He was always afraid of me.”

“Did he know you were a cold-blooded killer?”

One corner of his mouth curled upward in a smirk. “Doubt it. He was never that smart. But he was afraid of me. He always did what I told him to do.”

Dean walked into camp, fishing line empty. Silver was thankful to put an end to the exchange with Matt Carlton.

“No luck?” she asked the boy, although the answer was obvious.

“Nope.”

Carlton continued as if there’d been no interruption. “I’ll get off, you know. The law won’t be able to hold me. There isn't enough evidence, and I'll hire the best of attorneys to make sure I go free."

Dean whirled on the prisoner. "You won't get off. I know you done it. I know you killed my ma and pa."

"Did you see me do it, kid?"

Scowling, Dean shook his head.

"Then you don't know whether I did it or not."

Would Carlton get off? Would he go free for lack of evidence? The thought sickened Silver.

Jared guided the pinto down the mountain, moving slowly for the sake of the bay. If he remembered correctly, there were several farms outside of a small town in the valley to the north. He should be able to reach the first of them by two o'clock. The bay was a prime piece of horseflesh. The gelding would be as good as new after a week of rest. With any luck, Jared would be able to trade for a sound horse and be back at their camp by suppertime.

He tried not to think about leaving Silver and Dean alone with Carlton, especially not overnight. If anything happened to Silver or that boy . . .

He asked the horses for a little more speed.

Chapter 36

After an early supper, Dean joined Silver in the shade of a tall pine tree. He sat cross-legged on the ground amid the dried needles and pungent-smelling pinecones, a frown drawing his brows close together. "Do you think he's right?"

"Who?"

He jerked his head toward Carlton. "Him."

"About what?"

"Is he gonna get off like he says?"

Silver patted his knee. "He's just trying to convince himself. Shoring up his own confidence. That's all." *And I'm doing exactly the same thing now.*

"I ain't gonna let that happen. If he gets loose, I'll shoot him myself. If I have to follow after him like Mr. Newman's been doin', even if I have t' do it the rest of my life, I'll see that he hangs for what he done to my ma and pa. I swore it when Mr. Newman buried them."

Tears burned the back of her eyes. She hated seeing the boy in pain. "Don't let what happened harden your heart, Dean. It is you who will suffer because of it. Matt Carlton doesn't care what you feel about him. He won't lose a bit of sleep over it." She brushed the boy's hair off his forehead. "And it's needless to worry about what might happen when we get to Denver. We can't change it by worrying about it."

Dean scrambled to his feet. "I wish Mr. Newman had shot him back in Virginia City. Then we wouldn't have to worry about him goin' free."

"Oh, Dean. Don't say that. Wanting justice is one thing. Wanting to kill is another."

"Maybe, but it's what I want anyways." He turned and walked away.

Jared wasn't going to make it back before dark. The farmer, a crafty old buzzard, had dickered for what seemed an eternity. Not that the dickering changed the outcome. He'd been willing all along to make a fair trade. But the old man had seemed determined to draw out the process as much as possible. Maybe he'd been lonely and in need of a bit of company. Whatever the reason, Jared still had too much ground to cover before nightfall.

Once he was on his way, he pushed hard. Lather foamed on the horses' necks and hindquarters. The heat was unmerciful, even at this elevation. Shadows lengthened, the sun riding low behind him.

He didn't like the idea of Silver and Dean being in camp with Carlton after it grew dark. He'd told Silver to keep away from him, not to take any risks, not to move him for any reason. But he'd learned these past two months that Silver had a mind of her own. She didn't always do as she was told. He'd even come to appreciate her independent spirit. However, it also gave him cause to worry, and that worry gnawed at him as he pressed toward their campsite.

With a shout, Matt Carlton came to his feet. He shook one leg, then the other. "Ants! I'm crawling with ants!" He swore as he tried to bat at his pant legs with his cuffed hands, the chain rattling. "Get me out of here!"

Revolver in hand, Silver stepped forward. She half expected a trick, but he told the truth. They were the big, biting kind of ants. The insects swarmed around the base of the tree, and Carlton's boots and legs were covered with them.

"Do something! They're all over me."

Silver turned and ran across the camp. She set down the gun and picked up a saddle blanket, then raced back to him. Mindful to keep as much distance as possible between them, she swung the blanket against his legs and feet. Even as she did so, she felt as if the ants were beginning to swarm up her legs as well.

Carlton cursed again. "That's not doing any good. You've got to get me away from them. They're eating me alive."

Silver backed away, undecided. Tiny red welts had appeared on Matt Carlton's hands and forearms. There had to be more of them underneath his trousers and shirtsleeves. She couldn't just leave him there. It would be inhumane.

Jared's voice sounded in her head. *"Don't remove those handcuffs. Not for any reason . . . Not even if a forest fire blazes through here and burns him to a crisp."*

But she wouldn't be removing his handcuffs. He would still be cuffed and chained. All she would do was move his location. Surely she could do that without any risk. She'd observed Jared do it more than once.

"Dean, you're going to have to help me." She hurried toward the saddlebags, where she knew Jared kept the spare set of keys to the padlock.

"Mr. Newman said not to let him go, no matter what. You told me so yourself."

"I can't leave him where he is. The ants are biting. Even a man like him doesn't deserve that."

"Sure he does. He's done worse. Let 'em eat him."

Silver turned to look at the boy, the key in her hand. "But we aren't like him, Dean. We still know how to show another human being mercy. Even someone evil. Right?"

Dean didn't reply.

"Now help me. I can't do this alone."

"Mr. Newman ain't gonna like it."

No, Jared wouldn't like it. Not one bit.

"He'll know we didn't have any other choice."

She glanced over her shoulder. Carlton continued to curse as he swatted at the ants. What if it was her in his place? She shuddered at the thought. "We'll do it like Mr. Newman does it each morning. I'll keep the gun pointed at him while you slip the chain through the cuffs. Then we'll walk him to another tree and padlock the chain again."

It sounded simple enough. There'd never been a bit of trouble when Jared had done it. She had the Colt revolver, after all, and she knew how to use it. Besides, Carlton's hands would still be cuffed. What possible trouble could he be?

"You stay behind the tree," she reminded Dean as she picked up the revolver. With the barrel of the gun, she pointed to the opposite side of the camp. "We'll move him over there."

Together they walked toward Matt Carlton.

"About time," he snapped.

"Go on, Dean."

She leveled a steady gaze at her captive. "We're going to move you to that tree over there, but if you make any trouble, I'll shoot. Do you understand me? One wrong move and I'll shoot you dead."

He swore again.

"Dean." Silver nodded when the boy looked at her from beyond the tree. "Hurry before the ants get all over you too." She heard a click. A moment later, she saw the chain slacken. Her heart seemed to stop beating. She raised the revolver and pointed it at Carlton's chest, her finger on the trigger. "I don't care if they're biting you. You stand still until I tell you to move."

But once the chain was free of the tree, Matt Carlton began to hop and spin and swat and curse, pulling Dean along behind him at the opposite end of the chain.

"Stop, Carlton," Silver cried. "Stop now. I'll shoot." It surprised her when he obeyed. "Now get to that tree over there. To your right." She motioned with the gun barrel in the general direction she wanted him to go.

Carlton shot her an angry look but again obeyed. Dean followed at the end of the chain.

"Put your wrists against the tree," Silver told him. "Dean, you know what to do."

She began to relax. It was almost over. They'd done the merciful thing in moving the prisoner, and the transition had gone without a hitch. Jared would have done the same thing and gotten the same result.

Carlton made a sudden and unexpected move. He jerked the chain toward him, and Dean stumbled forward. Silver pulled the trigger. The force of the shot knocked her off balance. By the time she'd steadied herself, Carlton's arms were on either side of Dean's head, and the links connecting the handcuffs were pulled tightly against the boy's throat.

"Put down the gun, Silver."

She shook with fear, but she didn't lower it.

He tightened his hold on the boy's neck. "Put it down or I'll kill him where he stands."

"Next time I won't miss."

"But the boy'll still be dead. You can kill me, but it won't bring him back." He jerked on the cuffs. Dean's fingers came up to his throat, trying to pry himself free from the chain that choked him. The boy's face turned a bright red, and his eyes bulged. "Do it now or he's dead."

Ice trickled through her veins as she lowered the Colt revolver.

The campfire illuminated Carlton's form beneath the tree, and it looked like Silver and Dean were asleep in their bedrolls. But Jared's gut told him something was wrong. Then he knew what. He'd tied the prisoner to a different tree that morning. He wasn't in the right place. Carlton had been moved.

Jared dismounted. His gelding nickered. There was no response from the other horses. Jared's tension increased.

"Easy, boy." Jared drew his Colt from the holster. He entered the campsite, alert as he made his way toward the prisoner who was completely covered with the blanket, even his head. "Carlton," he said, voice low. "Wake up."

Carlton didn't move, so Jared nudged him with the toe of his boot. Still no response. Jared reached down with his free hand and yanked the blanket away. His heart slammed against his ribs. It wasn't Carlton beneath the blanket. It was Dean—bound, gagged, and cuffed to the tree. There was a cut along his temple, the blood now dried and crusty. The boy's expression was dazed. Whether from sleep or the knock he'd taken to his head, Jared didn't know.

He dropped to one knee. "Dean, what happened?" He freed the boy from the gag first.

"He got Silver."

"How long ago?"

The boy shook his head. "Don't know. It wasn't dark yet, I know that much. He hit me an' knocked me cold." His arms freed, he lifted fingers to touch the bloody spot at his temple.

"How did it happen?"

"It was my fault. We were movin' him 'cause there was ants bitin' him. They were all over him. I didn't care if they ate him alive, but Miss Silver said we couldn't just leave him there. Everything was goin' okay, but then he jerked me forward with the chain and got me around the neck. Said he'd kill me if she didn't put the gun down. She'd already shot at him once and missed. Guess she was afraid what he'd do to me if she tried again."

Jared stood. It was a miracle Carlton hadn't killed Dean before leaving the campsite. It wouldn't bother him for a moment to murder a child.

As if guessing Jared's thoughts, Dean said, "Before he knocked me out, he said to tell you that he'll kill her if you follow him."

Matt Carlton had left the boy alive to deliver that message. But Jared knew Carlton would kill Silver whether or not he followed. He had three, maybe four, hours' head start, and he'd had some of it in daylight.

With haste, Jared made a torch out of tree branches and a cloth. Then he moved toward where he'd left the remaining two horses that morning. Both of them were now gone. He hunkered down and peered at the ground but soon realized he needed more light than the torch provided in order to discover which way Carlton had gone with Silver. Even if they started off in the right direction, they could quickly go astray. Jared was an excellent tracker, but even he couldn't see in the dark.

Silver. Carlton had Silver. "God," he whispered, desperation welling in his chest, "don't let him hurt her. Please, please, God. Don't let him hurt her."

A small hand touched his shoulder. He looked up to find Dean, cheeks streaked with tears, standing beside him. "I'm sorry, Mr. Newman. It was my fault."

Jared pulled the boy close, taking and giving comfort with his embrace. "We'll get her back, Dean. We're going to get her back."

"Can we go now?"

"We'll have to wait. We have to be sure which way they went." Waiting for daylight. It would be one of the hardest things he'd done in his life. "We'll leave at first light."

Chapter 37

Silver swayed in the saddle. Pain shot tiny needles from her jaw where Carlton had struck her, and her right eye was nearly swollen shut. She was cold too, dressed only in her blouse and skirt. She longed to welcome the rising of the sun, although she knew she would despise it when the heat blasted down on them.

Jared is behind us somewhere. He's coming for me, and Carlton knows it.

Another wave of dizziness washed over her. She sank her fingernails into the leather pommel, refusing to let her fatigue and pain win this battle. She was safe as long as they kept moving. Once they stopped, there was no telling what he might do to her.

Jared will come. He'll find me.

But would he come in time? Or would he find only her body?

I should have told him I loved him. It was my pride that wanted him to say it first. And now it could be too late.

She glanced ahead toward the shadows that were Carlton and his mount. Her stomach sickened at the thought of him touching her. She would rather die.

No, I must live. I mustn't let Carlton take anything more from Jared. I must fight him and live. I must fight harder than I've ever fought anything.

She looked toward the eastern horizon and saw the approach of dawn. Once the sun was up, Carlton would force them to move faster. He was afraid of Jared. Whether he admitted it or not, he was afraid. Perhaps that was why he hadn't killed her yet. He needed her for protection. He needed someone to bargain with.

Hurry, Jared. Hurry.

Carlton reined in his horse. "We'll rest here." He dismounted and walked toward Silver and Cinder, his stiff movements revealing his own weariness and misery. "Come on. Get down." He untied the ropes that bound her wrists to the saddle horn, then grabbed her arm and yanked her from the saddle.

Her feet touched the ground, and her knees buckled.

He jerked his head toward some nearby brush. "I'll give you a little privacy. Try to go farther than that, and you'll rue the day."

She managed to rise and walk around the large bush. She took longer than necessary, as long as she dared, all the while thinking that every moment she delayed brought Jared that much closer.

When she returned to the horses, her legs feeling rubbery beneath her, Carlton held out a canteen. "Drink. We won't have time for food."

As she lifted the canteen to her parched mouth, she saw him watching the mountainside they'd just descended. Watching for Jared. Afraid. It made her want to smile.

Wordlessly, she returned the canteen to him.

Instead of taking it, he touched the bruise on the side of her face. "Do as I say and maybe I won't have to hit you again." Then he took the canteen from her hand before she dropped it.

Without being told, Silver returned to her horse. It took every ounce of her waning strength to pull herself into the saddle, but she did it. She didn't want Carlton touching her again.

Jared kept his horse alternating between a canter and a fast walk and spared no time for conversation with Dean. He knew the boy understood that he couldn't fall behind. Every minute counted. Carlton wasn't taking any trouble to cover his tracks. That either meant he wasn't worried about Jared catching up with him or he didn't know much about hiding out in the mountain terrain.

With every hoofbeat on rocky soil, Jared berated himself. He never should have left Silver alone with Carlton. It had been too great a risk. He'd known it but had gone anyway. At the very least, he should have taken the padlock key with him so Silver couldn't have used it. Why hadn't he thought to do so?

Panic clamored in his chest. He pushed it back.

Stay calm. Keep your mind clear.

If any harm came to Silver, it would be his fault. He'd left her with that killer and trusted her to obey his orders. He should have known better. When had Silver ever obeyed an order he'd given her without question, without asserting that stubborn will of hers? And he'd give anything to have her with him now, giving her opinion, showing her stubbornness, causing him grief. He wanted her with him until the day he died. He wanted the last words on his lips to be, "I love you, Silver."

He fought back the fear. He couldn't give in to it. He couldn't even think about Silver and how much he loved her and what it would do to him if he lost her. He couldn't think of anything now except following Carlton's tracks.

Carlton and Silver ate the last of the jerky and washed it down with cold water from a mountain stream. Silver tried to eat slowly, to savor every bite. She knew it might be a long while before she ate again. And each moment she delayed would bring Jared closer to her.

She sat on an outcropping of rocks beneath the

shade of a juniper tree. Cinder and the sorrel gelding grazed on sparse clumps of grass nearby. Behind her, she heard Carlton moving about. She twisted to look at him. He was staring back down the stretch of trail they'd climbed during the course of the afternoon.

Several times that day he'd changed direction. He pretended to know where they were going, but she was convinced he didn't. He'd yelled at her often, telling her to hurry, threatening her if she tried to hold them back. She'd denied his accusations but had continued to do anything she could to slow them down. A minute here, a few minutes there.

As she watched, Carlton began to pace from side to side, his movements quick and jerky, his shirt stained with sweat. He cursed as he moved, one moment his knuckles resting on his hips, the next flailing the air.

Be afraid, Matt Carlton. Be very afraid.

He spun toward her, as if she'd spoken the words aloud. "Get mounted. We're not stopping for the night yet."

She did as she was told, but after she was in the saddle, she looked behind her. Jared was out there. She knew it. She could feel him. He was coming for her.

Hunkered down, Jared traced his fingers over the sandy soil. "One of the horses lost a shoe.

The hoof's cracking. Could pull up lame. Might slow him down." He stood.

Dean held his hat in his hands. Grain filled the deep crown, and he fed it to one horse, then the other. "How far you figure we're behind 'em?"

"Two hours, maybe a bit less. They're not stopping to rest very often, but we're still moving faster. I don't think he knows where he's going. That's good. Uncertainty is good."

Dean shook the traces of grain and the horses' slobber from his hat, then placed it on his head. "I'm ready when you are."

The boy was tired, but he hadn't complained even once. Jared remembered how much Silver had hated the trail at first, but she'd been as tenacious as Dean was now. Carlton wasn't giving Silver much rest, but at least the man couldn't harm her while they were riding. Jared took some comfort in that knowledge.

Hang on, Silver. We're coming.

The sun had barely dipped beyond the horizon when Carlton stopped for the night. Even now, the heat of day lingered. The sky was a light pewter color. True darkness wouldn't come for hours, for already the full moon was a promise in the east.

They dismounted and Carlton ordered Silver to spread her blanket on the ground and lie down. He didn't have to tell her twice. Her weary legs seemed to crumple beneath her. Under the wool blanket, the sandy red soil was hard, but it mattered little to her. She was just glad to be down from the saddle.

With a sigh, she turned on her side, resting her head on the jacket Carlton had allowed her to pull from her saddle pack. Since her wrists were still bound together, she couldn't put it on, but she would be able to draw it over her shoulders as the night cooled. She could taste grains of sand in her teeth. She longed for a drink of water but decided not to ask. The less attention she called to herself the better.

She stiffened, her breath catching in her throat. Carlton had spread his own blanket next to hers. Even now he stretched out beside her. Terror dug its icy claws into her throat.

"Get some sleep. We're not staying the night. Just a couple hours. Then we push on. Try to get away and I'll shoot you. I've got the gun now." He chuckled softly. "I won't miss. I'm a better shot than you."

She lay still, listening as his breathing steadied, certain she wouldn't be able to sleep with him so close. But she was wrong. Exhaustion over-ruled fear.

Chapter 38

Silver came fully awake. Close behind her, Carlton's breathing was slow and even.

What had awakened her?

She opened her eyes and perused the mostly open ground before her. The promise of dawn had lightened the sky. There was no breeze, no sounds of scurrying nocturnal animals. Their horses stood nearby, heads hanging low as they slept.

Something had awakened her. What was it?

Jared.

Her pulse quickened as his name resounded in her heart. Jared was out there. He was out there this very moment. He wasn't following any longer, trying to find her. He was there now, watching her as night gave way to day. Should she try to roll away from Carlton? Should she try to get up and run?

Beside her, Carlton cursed, and she understood he was angry for sleeping through the night. She smiled to herself, thankful for his mistake.

Then something changed. He seemed to hold his breath. The air seemed to crackle with tension. Did he feel Jared's presence too?

The barrel of the gun pressed against the base of her skull. "If you don't do exactly what I say, I'll kill you. Understood?"

She had no chance of escaping him. Not yet.

"Get up nice and slow. Don't try any quick moves."

She didn't move.

"Now!" He shoved her with the gun, knocking her head forward. Then he took hold of her loose, tangled hair and pulled her head back toward him.

She sat up, sliding onto her knees, then stood. Without moving her head, she looked for Jared, but there was no one in sight. The ground was barren. The nearest trees and brush were a good fifty yards away. Behind them was a rocky trail and steep drop-off into a deep ravine.

Carlton pulled Silver backward, the revolver still touching her. "I won't let him take you alive. You might as well know it."

"You won't escape this time. You'll seal your fate the instant I'm dead. The sooner you kill me, the sooner you die too."

His fingers bruised her arm, and he cursed her.

Her heart thundered in her chest. Blood pulsed in her ears until she could scarcely hear anything else. She waited for the shot that would take her life, but the bullet didn't come. Carlton still needed a shield. It wasn't over yet. Not quite yet.

Jared peered down the barrel of his rifle, certain that Carlton didn't know exactly where Jared was, based on his jerky movements. Still the fugitive managed to keep Silver in the line of fire as he edged both of them toward more cover. If the sun was up, if the light was better, maybe Jared could have taken a shot, but as it was, he risked hitting Silver instead.

"What do we do?" Dean whispered.

Jared didn't look at the boy. "Don't move. Not a muscle," he answered. "You stay here until I tell you different. Understood?"

Instinct told him Dean nodded, but Jared never took his eyes off Carlton and Silver.

"I know you're out there, Newman," Carlton shouted. "Throw down your gun and show yourself."

Jared stayed quiet as he drew a slow, deep breath.

"I'll kill her, Newman. You know it and she knows it. You let us ride out of here without any trouble, you don't follow me any farther, and I'll let her go."

"You're a liar, Carlton. That's something else we all know. You let Silver go first, then we'll talk."

Carlton whipped Silver a step to the left and peered through the dim morning light in the direction of Jared's voice. "You're not the law. You got no right to take me anywhere."

"I've got the right. Nothing's changed about that."

"What am I worth to you, Newman? What's the

reward they're offering? I'll get the money myself and pay you off. I've got friends. I can get the money. I'll double it."

If Carlton took one wrong step, Jared might be able to stop him before he reached full cover. But he was moving with great care, no longer keeping himself sheltered behind Silver's body by dumb luck.

"How much, Newman?"

Money didn't mean a thing to Jared without Silver. If he lost her, he lost anything that mattered. No reward could change that. But that was something Matt Carlton would never understand.

As Jared watched through his rifle sight, Silver suddenly twisted around and shoved her captor. Then she bolted away from Carlton. The man pointed his gun after her, but Jared fired his rifle first. Carlton dropped. Jared took off running. He saw Carlton get to his feet again, holding the right side of his head and swaying as if drunk. The bullet must have grazed him and left him dazed. But Jared wasn't concerned with Carlton now. He'd lost sight of Silver. Where was she? Could she—

A scream reached his ears. Silver's scream.

Jared faltered, caught himself, ran faster even as he saw Carlton stumble toward his horse. Jared could stop him from getting away, or he could race to find Silver. He chose the latter.

• • •

The slide down the sharp incline had terrified Silver, but she was even more frightened by the narrowness of the ledge that held her now. Beyond it was a sheer drop to the bottom of the deep, rocky ravine. Certain death if she was to start to slide again. Her hands and arms were scraped and bleeding, the result of trying to stop her descent after she slipped and fell.

"Silver!"

She tipped her head back, trying to see Jared.

"Don't move. I'll get a rope."

"Carlton. Is he dead?"

"He's wounded, but he got away."

She closed her eyes. It was her fault Matt Carlton had escaped. All her fault. How could Jared ever forgive her?

"It doesn't matter, Silver. Don't move. I'll be back."

She obeyed him, holding as still as possible. Her heart jumped every time more dirt and rocks shifted and slid on either side of her. The passage of time seemed to slow to a crawl. An eternity passed before she heard the welcome sound of Jared's voice again.

"Grab ahold, Silver, and I'll pull you up."

Relief overwhelmed her as her hands tightened around the knot Jared had tied near the end of his lariat and thrown to her, and as she inched her way up the incline, tears of relief began to streak her cheeks.

The instant her head and shoulders rose above the ridge, Jared grabbed hold and hauled her the rest of the way up. Then he pulled her to him and buried his face in her hair.

"I knew you were coming," she whispered. "I knew you'd find me."

His hands cupped the sides of her face, forcing her head back so he could stare down into her eyes. His left hand slipped forward to tenderly touch the bruised and swollen skin on the right side of her face. "He hurt you."

"Only that. Nothing more."

"When I saw he'd taken you—"

"I knew you would come. I knew you wouldn't rest until you found me."

He kissed the wound above her eye. He kissed her forehead. He kissed the tip of her nose. "I never should have left you alone. I should have known you couldn't follow orders."

"I knew you'd come. I wasn't afraid as long as I remembered that."

"He could have shot you. He almost did."

"You shot him first."

And finally, he kissed her mouth, a lifetime of loving promised in the touch of his lips. "Why did you let him loose, even for a moment?"

"He was covered with ants. I couldn't leave him like that. I thought—"

"You promised you wouldn't."

"I had to."

"Why are you always so stubborn?" He offered another gentle kiss. "Look what almost happened. Look what *did* happen."

"I'm sorry you lost the reward because of me."

"Do you think it's the reward I care about?" His arms tightened around her, pulling her against his chest, one hand moving up and down her back, the fingers of the other twining through her hair. His next kiss branded her as his.

Silver melted into his embrace.

He withdrew slightly and stared down into her face. Then, with six simple words, he changed her world forever. "I love you, Silver. Marry me."

Chapter 39

Matt Carlton didn't escape justice. They came upon his body before they'd traveled more than a couple of miles. Although no one could say for certain what had happened, it appeared he'd fallen and struck his head when attempting to jump his horse over a tree that lay across the trail, barring his way. They found the sorrel gelding not far beyond, its reins tangled in the branches.

Jared wrapped Carlton's body in a blanket and draped him over the horse's back. Then they set off for the nearest town with a sheriff to whom they could tell their story, leave Matt Carlton to be buried, and go on their way.

There wouldn't be a trial. There wouldn't be a hanging. There wouldn't be a reward. And oddly enough, none of it mattered to Jared. All that mattered was the woman riding beside him. She and the boy too, surprising as that was.

The ragtag threesome arrived in Twin Springs in early August. The main street of town was dry and dusty, baked beneath the summer sun. A few horses stood outside the Mountain Rose Saloon, their tails flicking at persistent flies. Laundry had been strung up to dry behind the Mitchell home, and the Pearson boys were splashing in a tub of water while their mother rocked her new baby in the shade of the side porch.

All the familiar sights looked good to Silver. It felt as if she'd been gone years instead of not quite three months. Still, as they approached the mercantile, anxiety balled in her stomach. She'd sent her parents a telegram, letting them know she was okay and on her way back. But how were they going to receive the rest of the news she had yet to tell them? On the trail, it had been easy to think only of Jared and their love, but that interlude was over. She must tell her father and stepmother that the store and house were lost. She must face their disappointment.

She glanced toward Jared. He met her gaze

and offered a reassuring smile. He was with her, the look seemed to say. What more could she need? Nothing. That was enough. She looked to her opposite side and found Dean watching her too. His eyes were filled with uncertainty, and it was her turn to offer encouragement with a confident nod.

They reined in their horses in front of Matlock Mercantile. Silver stared up at the bold lettering across the false front. It seemed a lifetime since she'd last looked upon it. Maybe it had been a lifetime. She'd been another person. She had left Twin Springs a wounded woman in pursuit of a thief and had returned with her heart made whole again. More than whole. Made new.

The store door flew open, and her father stepped outside. "Silver! Thank God."

Her trepidation vanished, and she vaulted from the saddle, flying into his waiting arms. "Papa. Oh, Papa, it's good to be home." She buried her face against his burly chest.

"We've been worried about you, daughter."

She stepped back and looked into his eyes. She saw tears glimmering there and felt her resolve not to cry weaken. "I haven't brought good news, Papa. I wasn't able to get the money or Mother's jewelry back. It's all gone."

"You're home safe. That's all your mother and I wanted. Just that you would return to us unharmed. When we learned you didn't go to stay with Rose—" His words broke off, choked by emotion.

Jared stepped onto the boardwalk, and her father released his hold on Silver's arms.

"Mr. Newman. Silver was with you all this time?"

"Yes. Most of it."

Her father's gaze returned to her. "If anything had happened to you, Silver, it would have broken my heart. You shouldn't have gone the way you did. The store and house mean nothing compared to you. Don't you know that?"

"I had to try to get your money back, Papa. It was my fault."

"It wasn't your fault. Don't ever think it again." Once more he looked at Jared. "Thank you for bringing her home safe and sound, Mr. Newman." He offered his hand. "Thank you is a mighty small reward for bringing Silver back to us."

Jared shook the proffered hand, surprise written in his eyes. Neither of them had anticipated he would receive a warm welcome from her parents.

"Papa, there's something—"

The door opened a second time.

"Look, Marlene. Mr. Newman has brought Silver back to us."

"Silvana." Her stepmother came out onto the boardwalk. "At last."

Silver kissed her stepmother's cheek. "I'm back, Mother, but without the money. By the time we found Bob, it was already gone, and he was dying. We . . . we had to bury him in Nevada."

Her stepmother didn't seem to hear her last words. "We? You and this man found him?" Her complexion turned ashen.

Jared stepped to Silver's side, placing the palm of one hand against the small of her back. "Mrs. Matlock, I don't know if you remember me."

"I remember you, Mr. Newman."

"I want to reassure you that your daughter's reputation is intact. Nothing inappropriate passed between us. But it is our wish to be married."

"Married?" Her stepmother's exclamation brought color back to her cheeks. "You must be joking."

Silver stood a little straighter. "We are not joking, Mother. We love each other."

"Love? What do you know of love?"

Her father laid a hand on his wife's shoulder. "Marlene. Be quiet. This isn't the time or place."

"I will not be quiet. I will say what I—"

"Not another word, Marlene. I mean it."

Never had Silver heard such an authoritative tone when her father spoke to his wife. It surprised both women.

Jared cleared his throat in the awkward silence. "Mr. Matlock, I have come to love your daughter very much. I promise you, she won't marry a bounty hunter. That part of my life is behind me. She will have a home. We may never have much in the way of material things, but we will find a place to build our life together." He looked at Silver. "A place to raise horses or cattle. A place to raise our children, God willing."

Silver felt as if her heart had taken wing. Being cherished by Jared made her strong and courageous. She turned around and motioned Dean toward her. He came nervously, hands shoved into his trouser pockets.

"Dean, Jared and I have been talking, and we have something we want to ask you. After we're married, we would like to adopt you. We want to be a family, the three of us. What do you think?"

"Who is that boy?" her stepmother whispered.

Silver ignored her, intent on getting Dean's answer.

At last he spoke. "You want to be my ma?"

"Yes." She smiled.

"I'd stay with you and Mr. Newman for good?"

"Yes." Her smile broadened.

Dean glanced at Jared and then back to her. "I'd like it, Miss Silver. I'd like it a lot."

The wedding was a quiet affair held in the Matlocks' front parlor with only the family present. The bride wore a gown of pale pink with a garnish of rosebuds in her hair, which was worn loose about her shoulders. The bride's step-mother wept softly throughout the ceremony. Her father, on the other hand, beamed with joy.

Rose and Dan Downing stood up with the couple, and Dean, with the air of authority of an older cousin, kept an eye on the two Downing boys.

Jared—feeling uncomfortable in the suit, white collar, and necktie—took it all in, memorized it, treasured it. His new life had begun in earnest this day.

"You may kiss your bride," the minister said at long last.

Jared turned toward Silver, but he paused before taking her into his arms. Instead he withdrew something from his pocket and held it toward her.

Silver's eyes widened. "Great-Grandmother's locket? But you sold it."

"No." He shook his head. "I never sold it. I couldn't. It meant too much to you."

"Oh, Jared." She spoke his name in a whisper. "Thank you."

He stared down into her beautiful face and knew that God had blessed him above all men on earth. When he leaned in and kissed her, he hoped she might know the depth of his love for her. "Hello, wife," he said when he ended the kiss at last.

She smiled. "Hello, husband."

Then they turned to face their witnesses. That was when Jared saw Rick Cooper standing near the parlor doorway. When had he slipped into the room? How had the sheriff known about the wedding? Not that it had been a secret, but a wedding in Twin Springs wasn't exactly news in Denver.

Rick grinned and moved toward the couple. "Couldn't you let a friend know when you do something like this?"

"Sorry, Coop. It all came together rather fast."

"Could I talk to you in private a moment?"

"Now? This is my wedding, you know."

"It's important, and I think you'll want to hear it."

"Well, if you say it's important." Jared turned and kissed Silver again. "Coop, you remember my bride."

"I sure do." Rick nodded his head. "How do, Mrs. Newman?"

Silver's smile seemed to brighten the entire room. "I am well, Sheriff Cooper. Thank you for joining us."

Rick said, "I won't keep your groom more than a few minutes. I promise." He turned on his heel and led the way out of the parlor.

Jared followed close behind, wondering what had brought the sheriff all this way.

Rick stopped on the front porch and turned toward Jared.

"What's wrong, Cooper?"

"Nothing's wrong, but I have something for you."

The Lute Peterson reward. The paperwork must finally have been untangled.

Rick Cooper reached into his breast pocket. "This came for you to my attention." He pulled a folded slip of paper from his pocket. "It's from a Mr. Harrison in Fort Worth. When you telegraphed him about Matt Carlton's capture and death, you didn't tell him where you could be reached. You only said you were headed to Denver. So he arranged for this to come to the sheriff's office in hopes someone would know where to find you."

"Owen Harrison sent something to you?" Jared took the paper, unfolded it, saw what was inside. His jaw dropped. "But this is a bank draft for five thousand dollars."

"That's right."

"But I didn't bring Matt Carlton in. He didn't have to stand trial. I didn't prove he was the one who—"

"Maybe not, but Harrison wanted you to have the money anyway. He believes you caught his wife's killer. The sheriff in Utah confirmed the man's body had a crescent-shaped scar. That was proof enough for Mr. Harrison."

"But—"

"Just be thankful for it, Jared. You earned it."

"There's trouble of some sort, isn't there?" Silver's stepmother twisted a handkerchief in her hands. "I knew it. I knew something would go wrong if you married a bounty hunter. What else could you expect when—"

"Marlene," her father said. "Enough."

Her stepmother pressed her lips together, forming a thin line.

Silver was thankful for the cessation of her stepmother's comments, but she did wonder why the sheriff was there. Did he have a job for Jared, another criminal for him to track down? Jared had said he was giving up that way of life. He'd talked of heading north into Montana, but they had no money to speak of. If he took one more job, then he might take another and another. If he—

The door opened and Jared strode inside. Without a word he picked her up in his arms and spun around several times. When he set her down again, he kissed her. Thoroughly, enthusiastically kissed her, leaving her breathless.

"Jared, what on earth?"

"This! This is what on earth." He held out a bank draft. "Look at it."

It wasn't the size of the draft she noticed so much as the sense of relief that flowed through her. He wasn't going to buckle on his gun belt and ride off after another killer or bank robber.

Jared turned toward his in-laws. "Mr. and Mrs. Matlock, we have enough money to pay your mortgages. You won't have to leave your home or give up the store."

Stunned silence gripped the parlor. Her father and stepmother stared at Jared, then at each other, then back at Jared again.

Finally, her father said, "We can't ask you to do that. We have no right to it."

"You haven't asked. I want to do it." Jared put his arm around Silver's shoulders and drew her against his side. "*We* want to do it. There's enough to clear your debt and to set us up in a place of our own with a bit left over for the future."

"I don't know how much that reward is, son," her father continued, "but it could make your life much easier if you kept it for yourself and your family. We can't—"

"Mr. Matlock, there's something you don't understand. You're my family now. And besides . . ." Jared faced Silver again and stared into her eyes. "I've already got my reward."

Something warm and wonderful blossomed in Silver's chest as she returned his gaze.

Jared gathered her close, so close their two hearts seemed to beat as one. "I've already collected the greatest bounty of all. I've got my bounty of Silver."

A Note to Readers

Dear friends:

The Heart's Pursuit is a departure from my usual Americana settings where most of my historical romances take place. And though my regular readers will find it a different style, I hope, whether you are a new reader or someone who has read all of my books, you've enjoyed the chase across hundreds of miles with two people who needed to find each other far more than they needed to catch a fugitive.

Please note that the term *bounty hunter* was not in use at the time of this story. The first known use of the term was in 1930. But Hollywood started using the term in movies many of us watched as kids, and because of it, bounty hunters and Westerns became entwined in our collective minds. The bounty hunter became a part of folk-lore. I decided not to fight what felt so natural and so took creative license when writing this novel. I would love to hear from you. Please join me on:

Facebook
(https://www.facebook.com/robinleehatcher)

or Twitter
(https://twitter.com/robinleehatcher)
or some of the other social media.

For readers who sign up for my newsletter, sent four to six times a year, I offer a free PDF of my short story "The Huckleberry Patch." Just visit my website at http://www.robinleehatcher.com to sign up.

And if you like the book enough to take a moment to leave a review on Goodreads or Amazon or some other book site, please know how much I appreciate it. Also, please know that I've prayed for you—that what I've written will entertain while at the same time draw you one step closer to an awesome God who loves you with an extraordinary love.

In the grip of His grace,
Robin Lee Hatcher

❧ Reading Group Guide ❧

1. Which character in *The Heart's Pursuit* do you most relate to, if any? Why or why not?

2. What is the major theme of the book? What is it you will remember most about this story?

3. How did the Civil War, which ended eight years before this book opens, impact Jared's and Silver's families? In what ways were the protagonists still carrying the weight of those experiences?

4. Jared has to let go of the need for revenge. Have you ever desired revenge? If so, how did you move beyond that desire?

5. Silver has come to believe she isn't deserving of love. Have you ever felt that way? What does God say about His love for you?

6. Jared and Silver meet many different characters during their journey. Is there one you wish you could have known more about? Who is it and why?

7. *The Heart's Pursuit* takes place over a couple thousand miles, a very different setting from

the usual small-town settings favored by the author. Did you feel like you were crossing the country with the characters? Are you familiar with the parts of Colorado, Wyoming, Utah, and/or Nevada where the book takes place?

8. Are you familiar with other Robin Lee Hatcher novels? How does this novel compare? Can you name a favorite Hatcher novel?

About the Author

ROBIN LEE HATCHER is the best-selling author of seventy books. Her numerous awards include the Christy Award for Excellence in Christian Fiction, the RITA Award for Best Inspirational Romance, and the RWA Lifetime Achievement Award. Robin and her husband currently reside in Idaho. For more information, visit www.robinleehatcher.com.

Center Point Large Print
600 Brooks Road / PO Box 1
Thorndike ME 04986-0001 USA

(207) 568-3717

US & Canada:
1 800 929-9108
www.centerpointlargeprint.com